THINE OWN SELF

A Coming Out Novel

Ryan Provencher

Caulfield Publishing
Los Angeles, CA

Publisher's Note: This is a work of fiction. Characters, places, names and incidents are a creation of the author. Certain locations are real but used fictitiously to create atmosphere. Any resemblance to actual people living or dead or to businesses, companies or events is coincidental.

Special thanks to Mandy Moore for permission to use lyrics from her single, "Extraordinary" from her 2007 album, *Wild Hope.*

Cover photo by Hannah McCharen
Cover design created by Angie Zambrano
Author photo by Matt Baume

Thine Own Self / Ryan Provencher 1st edition
ISBN-13: 9780991545209
ISBN-10: 0991545206
Library of Congress Control Number: 2014903403
Ryan Provencher, Reseda, CA

For all those who have come out. You are the heroes. You are the ones who will change the world.

"Every gay person must come out. As difficult as it is, you must tell your immediate family. You must tell your relatives. You must tell your friends if indeed they are your friends. You must tell the people you work with. You must tell the people in the stores you shop in. Once they realize that we are indeed their children, that we are indeed everywhere, every myth, every lie, every innuendo will be destroyed once and all. And once you do, you will feel so much better."

Harvey Milk

ACKNOWLEDGEMENTS

Writing a first book can be extremely difficult. It was my editor and mother that helped turn this novel into what it is today. Words cannot express my gratitude for her help and guidance. I would also like to thank my father, brother, grandparents, and my entire extended family for all their support. Thanks must also go out to my friends Marina, Steve O., Rubén, Robert H., Marc, Judd, Brian, Richard, Ryan J, Hannah, Andrew B, and Patti H. Your friendship during my coming out and in writing this book has been invaluable. Lastly, I must thank the most important person in my life, my husband, Scott. His love, support and guidance throughout this process has been amazing. I could never have written this book without him.

CHAPTERS

All chapter quotations are from Shakespeare. Please refer to the last pages of the book for references.

A NOTE FROM THE AUTHOR

For years I've loved the words of William Shakespeare. When I was introduced to his plays in high school, they would pull me in and never let go. It was in my senior year when my English teacher made reference to Hamlet's "What a piece of work is man" soliloquy that I was prompted to recite it to her. She was extremely impressed. I never confessed that I learned it from Captain Jean Luc Picard in a *Star Trek* episode.

There is still such relevance in Shakespeare's words penned hundreds of years ago that I borrowed from the master for the chapter titles of this book. When it came to choosing the title for this novel, I went to Polonius' fatherly advice to his son Laertes: "This above all: To thine own self be true". I believe the only way for me to be a completely comfortable gay man is to be true to myself and happy with the person I am.

It is my hope that this novel will in some way help others with the coming out process while also giving straight people insights into just how difficult it can still remain for this generation.

PROLOGUE

"The fault…is not in our stars, but in ourselves"

I hate myself. Why is it that every time I walk into the school locker room I'm terrified? I can't even take a shower because I don't want to be around all those naked guys. It makes me crazy, and on top of that, I have to deal with the fact that most nights all I do is dream about those same damn guys. My best friend Chris caught me off guard the other day as I was rushing out of the locker room.

"Hey, Brad, wait up," he calls running after me.

"What's up, Chris?" I reply quickly as I turn to face him.

Already I know what the question's going to be. There's no way I'm going to be able to avoid the fact that in almost four years of high school, I haven't once taken a shower with the rest of the guys. Usually I manage to get out of the gym quick enough or have some lame excuse that I need to get home right away.

"Hey, you trying out for track next year or maybe you're one of those superheroes in disguise?" he questions with a smirk. Chris' got one of those classic smirks that girls seem to find so endearing and damn it all, so do I.

"No? Huh? What are you talking about?" I stammer, fidgeting with my car keys.

"Jesus, man, with the way you were bolting out of there, I thought you were either trying out for cross country or had the runs," he laughs. Chris always seems to find the perfect thing to say that can make you cringe and blush.

"Nah, just got a lot of stuff to do and I need to get out of here," I answer.

Man, I just have to keep avoiding the chance of having the topic brought up and then I'm home free.

"And so what are you doing this weekend, Romeo?" I ask. "Another date with Sarah?" I've gotta keep pushing the conversation on him so we're off the "locker room topic."

"Yeah, I guess so. I still can't believe I decided to go out with her simply because of those thirty-eight Ds. We were making out in my car the other day and my hand slipped on the seat. Geez, I lost my balance and my head fell right into her boobs. I thought I was never going to get out of there. I almost passed out. 'Air, gimme air, I screamed,'" he explains clutching his throat and laughing.

Okay. Thank god we can talk about normal stuff like girls. Normal guy stuff. Yeah, right. I remember a few weeks back when I was in my bedroom looking through my high school sophomore yearbook, checking out all the girls. I come from a little town in New Hampshire, and as you can imagine most of the girls are pretty much the same. I mean the state's filled with white bread protestant or Catholic girls who act all innocent to their mommies and daddies, but can be crazy outside the white picket fences. Okay, so they're not all like that, but I'd go with a strong 90 to 95 percent. Honest. Well, anyway, I was looking at all the attractive girls and none of them were doing anything for me. I mean all I needed was just a little reaction from below the waist, nothing big (no pun intended). Just something. You see, I seem to get aroused for no reason at all sometimes, but nothing seems to happen with girls. Oh, it's not that they don't notice me. I mean, I'm an okay looking guy. I'm about five nine, kind of lanky but I do work out some. I've got blond hair and blue eyes. I mean that should be enough to drive the opposite sex wild and they do notice and even flirt sometimes, but I never seem to make that right connection. I mean why me?

"Why me?" Chris asks for the third time giving me a gentle shove against a row of lockers.

"Um, hello? I'm opening up to you here, buddy. I mean I'm telling you my deepest darkest dating secrets and you're not even listening when you should be taking notes. Someday, my friend, your face is going to fall into some pretty deep cleavage and you'll wish you'd listened to me," he says laughing.

"Yeah, sorry. I've been a little out of it lately." Crap it's been way more than lately. I've gotta find a way to figure this out without anyone knowing. Now therein lies the rub. Hey, Hamlet, you may have been pretty messed up but at least you got a rise out of Ophelia.

"Hey, it's cool, Brad. I get it. Text me. We'll catch a movie or something this weekend," Chris responds in his usual reassuring voice.

"Yeah, sounds good," I sigh.

Sighing seems to be about the only thing I'm pretty good at doing lately.

The only bright light I seem to have in my future is for a summer high school internship. I called this guy, Harvey Bobson, the other day to see if his company needed interns for the summer. I saw an ad on-line. I gave up on getting any leads from guidance about three weeks ago. Their idea of a summer spent in film is developing rolls of 35mm stuff at the local drug store chain and I'm not even sure they still do that anymore. All digital. When I talked to Bobson, he said his company shoots all the NASCAR races in the state. Now normally I'd rather watch an egg fry on pavement on a fall day in New England than watch NASCAR racing, but, hey, it's a chance to work on a film, okay, video set, for the summer. It'll also give me the chance to get out of town for a little bit. You see, I've always wanted to work on movies. I've loved them since I was a little kid. I guess it's the idea of being able to get out of the world and escape in a dark theater. Anyway, shooting videos of cars racing around in a circle won't be the next Spielberg epic, but at least it's a step in the right direction.

Beep. Beep. Beep. God, I hate that frickin' alarm clock.

"Brad, come on. It's time to get up. I'll make pancakes if you get ready now," mom yells up to me. My mom has a tendency to bribe me with food and it usually works.

I have to say I'm more than a little lucky in the mom and dad department. They're the most supportive parents in the world. I'm an only child so I'm sure that comes into play. Actually, if truth be told, I did have an older brother. His name was Sean, but I never knew him. He died in a car accident. It had been raining and the damn driver was going too fast on slick roads and slammed into my parents' car. It spun all over the place and ended up flipping over. My brother, who was six at the time, smashed his head on the rear side window. There were no side-airbags back then so there was nothing to protect him. By the time they got the Jaws of Life in there, he was already dead. Thank god my parents were okay, but what's really hard for me is I never knew my brother. I was only a few months old at the time and I wasn't even in the car. My grandparents were watching me. I know losing Sean is the reason my parents are a little overprotective of me, but actually it doesn't bother me all that much. It shows they care. I mean I'm sure a lot of parents would have just given up after losing a child, but it seems they took their love for Sean and made it even greater for me. That's one of the reason's I can't ever tell them all the stuff I'm going through. I know they'll understand and I'm sure they'll be supportive, but I can't put them through anything else. It just wouldn't be fair. They've gone through enough.

"Brad, would you please get your butt downstairs? You're going to be late for your interview," mom calls, a lot more forcefully than before.

"Mom, I'm meeting the guy at Waffle Barn and I'm sure there'll be plenty of food there," I reply sarcastically, but playfully. My mom and I usually read each other pretty well.

"All right, smart ass, but at least get down here so we can chat before you go."

Bolting down the stairs, I notice my hands shaking nervously. Once in the kitchen, she puts her hands on my shoulders and dispenses her motherly advice which I sort of need right now.

"Okay, now be sure to make a good impression, Brad. I know you always do, but in the end just be yourself and I'm sure you'll be fine," she says pushing my hair back in place.

The Waffle Barn isn't that far from my house so I'm a little early. Hey, I knew I had plenty of time. As I walk into the restaurant, I try to stand up straighter so I look a little taller. At a little under five foot nine, I need all the help I can get. Hopefully I look much more confident than I am. I don't really have a resume, but my dad said I probably didn't need one. I really didn't have time to get one together anyway with all these crazy projects my teachers seem to keep tossing out in almost every subject. Without anything in my hands though, I'm trying my best to resist the urge to wring them together like some character from a B movie.

"Bradley?"

The voice comes from behind me. I almost don't turn around as my mother and grandmother are the only ones that call me that.

"Um, yes," I say exuding as much confidence as I can muster.

"Hi. I'm Harvey Bobson. Nice to meet you."

Harvey reaches out his hand and I take it, noting his grasp is a little stronger than I'm used to. Harvey's a big guy—a lot taller and heavier than I am. Like a lot of guys his age, he's got a gut from drinking too many beers while sitting in front of the TV watching ball games most weekends. His grey hair is dyed a little too dark and can't begin to disguise the fact that he's at least fifty. I get the impression he's trying to make himself more important than he is. But, hey, isn't that what I'm trying to do.

"So let's get some food and talk about the internship," he says with a smile that seems genuine, I suppose.

"Sure, sounds good to me, Mr. Bobson," I reply wondering whether I'll even be able to eat with my stomach churning like it does before mid terms.

"Please, please, call me Harvey," he replies, patting me on the shoulder like we've been pals for years.

Following the hostess to the table, I notice he's walking behind me which for some reason seems odd. Isn't he supposed to be the one running this interview, but hey, what do I know about this kind of stuff.

"So tell me, son," I hate it whenever anyone but my dad or grandfather calls me son. It seems like some kind of ownership they don't really have. "Just why are you interested in working with my company?"

"Well, I've always wanted to work in the movie business and this seems like a great place to start," I reply.

This is the answer I've been running through in my head all the way over here, but somehow it doesn't sound anywhere near as good as it did in the confines of my '08 Altima. Reaching into my pocket, I pull out my diabetic tester.

You see, I'm an insulin dependent diabetic and I have to check my blood sugar before eating anything. I hate having to take it out during the interview, but I really have no choice.

Harvey sees me doing it and looking intrigued asks, "So, you're a diabetic?"

"Um, yeah, been for years, but I keep it in really good control and it wouldn't affect anything dealing with the work I'd have to do," I stammer. I'm never quite sure how people will respond to my having diabetes.

"No, no. Please don't worry about that. I was just making conversation," he replies with a concerned voice that seems genuine, but I'm really having a hard time reading this guy.

For the next thirty minutes or so we discuss what the job will entail while I eat some scrambled eggs with toast and some o.j.

"Since the races don't happen everyday, we do some other shooting as well around the area. We sometimes do videography of assembly meetings and things like that. Does this sound like something you'd be interested in being a part of?" he asks.

"Of course, Mr. Bobson. Any chance to learn more about the process would be incredibly helpful to me," I say with as much excitement in my voice as I can muster.

The rest of the interview seems to go okay, but as we get up to leave the restaurant, I tell him I need to use the men's room.

"Yeah, me too. Lead on."

I'm not sure what I hate more, rest rooms or locker rooms, but after I'm finished doing my business, I catch Harvey looking me up and down.

"Have you done any modeling before?" he says looking absolutely serious.

"Are you kidding?" I say with a half nervous laugh.

"No, no. I really think you could do modeling in some local ads. Now do me a favor and stand up straight," he says smiling while continuing to look me over.

I do as I'm told. I'm good at that. I tend to be a pretty good kid who doesn't seem to get in much trouble, but I'm starting to get really uncomfortable as his eyes continue to roam. I've never had anyone look at me like this, but, hey, he probably knows more about who could make it as a model than I do.

Finally he stops with all the wandering eyes and tells me I should really consider modeling and goes on and on about how great I'd be at it. Leaving the rest room, he touches my shoulder, telling me he has a few more questions about the things he's looking for in an intern and whether it would be okay to continue the interview in his car since he needs to run to a pharmacy up the street to pick up some pictures. I mean, I really want to get this internship so what the heck. As he unlocks the car, I can't help but notice the crap all over the place. And I thought my car got messy. He casually tosses magazines, papers and water bottles onto the back seat, giving me some room up front.

"Sorry about the mess. I didn't expect to have anyone in the passenger seat today," he says apologetically as he tosses a fast food wrapper into the back.

Driving down Route 93 he makes small talk, like what are my favorite movies, what kinds of music do I like, and all that kind of stuff. Suddenly I realize we've been driving for a long time, maybe twenty minutes or so, and have crossed the border into Massachusetts.

As politely as I can and trying really hard to disguise the nervousness in my voice, I manage to ask how much longer it's going to be before we get to the pharmacy.

"Geez. Sorry about that. I didn't realize it was going to take this long. We should be there in a sec," he replies with a quick glance over to me.

Now I'm really starting to get nervous. I don't even know what city we're in only that we've passed that big sign that announces "Welcome to Massachusetts." But then again this guy hasn't really done anything yet that's bad. I mean, at least I don't think so.

As we pull into the Your-Aid parking lot, he gets out of the car and says he'll be right back. Waiting, I check my cell and realize the battery's dead. Damn, I should have joined Boy Scouts like my parents suggested. At least then I'd know how to be prepared.

After about five minutes, Harvey slides into the driver's seat and tosses me the bag with the photos.

"Check 'em out, Bradley. Not bad, huh? I'm just getting into portrait shots and I think I'm getting pretty good."

Glancing at the photos, I notice they're all of young kids and I'm getting really uneasy. I can't kid myself any longer. This guy's really freaking me out explaining that in addition to his work with the speedway, he really enjoys getting kids into modeling. I try to remain calm as we pull out of the parking lot, but back onto the highway, the frightening questions begin.

"So, Bradley, as a diabetic do you have any problems getting an erection?" he asks in a creepily calm voice.

Taken off guard, I just sit there in silence for what seems like an eternity. Finally I stammer, "Um, what?"

"Well, when I was younger, I used to work in the adult entertainment industry and we had a diabetic actor who always had issues getting it hard and I was just wondering if you have that kind of problem," he continues, faking real concern.

"That's...uh...not really a question I'm comfortable answering," I quickly reply.

Man, I just need to get home. Thank god we're almost back at the restaurant where my car's parked.

Harvey quickly apologizes, saying he thought we had started to become friends and it'd be okay to ask something a little more personal. The fact of that matter is his apology means nothing to me. The guy's a creep and I need to get the hell out of this car.

Pulling into a space at the far side of the parking lot, I realize how far away we are from the rest of the cars. Reaching for the handle, I hear the click of the automatic lock as I fumble to find the damn release button.

"What's your rush, Bradley?" he asks with a smirk I can only connect with the sleaziest character I've ever seen on film.

"Um, I really think I should be going," I stammer as I finally locate the unlock button and hear the click again.

Reaching again for the door handle, I feel his hand slid over my knee. As I quickly push away, he grabs the back of my neck hard and pulls my head towards his and says, "Believe me, kid, you're going to like this."

He starts kissing me full on the lips. Oh, my god, my first kiss with a guy and he's forcing it on me. Suddenly I'm overwhelmed with hate, revulsion and complete fear. I hate him, I hate me; I hate this whole damn world. I open my mouth a little and he responds giving me the chance to bite him hard on the lower lip. He quickly pushes me away and raising his right arm hitting me full in the face with his elbow. Completely terrified, I grab a pen from the console and jab it into his right thigh. As he screams in pain, I elbow him in stomach and push him towards his door, away from me. Grabbing my stuff, I leave Harvey Bobson, or whoever the hell he really is, and his kiddy porn in the far corner of the Waffle Barn parking lot.

As I walk into the house, my mom runs up to me with deep concern in her eyes, asking me what happened. It seems mothers have some sort of sixth sense when it comes to knowing their kids are in danger. Mustering up some fake sense of calm, I blow it off saying the guy was a jerk and when I told him I wasn't interested in the internship, he called me an ungrateful, spoiled brat and hit me in the face. Immediately my dad, who had just walked in from work, grabs the phone to call the police.

"I'm going to make sure that bastard gets what's coming to him. Hello, officer, yes…"

I decide not to fight my dad on this one, even though I'm more than a little afraid of what might come from it. While my dad's talking to the police, my mom keeps hugging me, trying to assure me that everything's going to be okay.

After all the parental craziness ends, I retreat to my room gently holding an ice pack to my face. My room is where I need to be right now. More than anything I need to lie down and close my eyes for a few minutes and forget about that damn pervert. Setting the ice pack on my desk, on top of the tee shirt I threw there this morning, I close my eyes and doze off. Immediately I'm in Harvey's car again. I can't see the face of the driver, but I know it's him and I know I have to get out of there or he's going to hurt me again, but when the driver's head turns, it's Chris's face. What the hell!

Chris is staring into my eyes and saying in an almost sing-song voice, "I know you've wanted this for a long time, Brad. Don't worry. It's okay. I feel the same way."

He reaches over and starts to caress my hair. I like the way it feels and I reach to touch his. Slowly Chris leans over and pulls my head towards his and we kiss passionately. I can't believe I'm kissing my best friend in the Waffle Barn parking lot. Chris slowly moves his hand to my chest, gradually moving it up as he gently touches my face.

"You're a great friend, Brad, and I want to be with you," he whispers into my ear.

And I want to be with him. Looking at him now with his soft features and smile that has always hypnotized me, I know this is what I've longed for. I want him to be the first.

"Brad, Brad, Bradley!"

Suddenly everything changes as I'm abruptly jolted out of my dream. It's not Chris talking, but my mother. My eyes snap open at the sound of her voice calling me from downstairs. Getting out of bed, I notice what I hate more than anything. The sheets are wet – another damn wet dream.

I really can't take this anymore. Now I'm dreaming about my god damn best friend, something I've never thought about before even in my craziest fantasies. There's way too much shit going on. I can't deal with it. I feel my face getting hot and I'm sure I'm turning red.

But what if all the gay people I meet are like Harvey Bobson? Fuck, I don't want to like guys. I want to be normal like my friends and almost everybody else at my school. The few gay guys there get the crap kicked out of them all the time and are constantly hassled. Everyone seems to say that it's getting better, but there's still a hell of a lot of harassment that adults just don't see or don't care to see. I just don't want to be...gay. I start to cry and can't seem to stop.

Mom calls up to me again, this time with a little more insistence.

"Honey, the food's going to get cold if you don't come down now," she calls.

"I'll be right down, Mom. I promise."

I take a deep breath and walk to my computer and start typing.

> *Dear Mom and Dad,*
> *I'm sorry I'm typing this letter and not writing it,*
> *but I didn't want to make any mistakes. I just can't*
> *handle this anymore. Today, when I had the "issue"*
> *with Mr. Bobson, it confirmed the very thing I hate*
> *most about myself. For a long time I've tried to hide*
> *the feeling that I think I like guys and not girls. I*
> *hate myself for feeling this way. All I want to do*
> *is wake up in the morning and like girls and live*

a normal life like everyone else. I don't want to be gay and I'm so afraid that's what's going to happen to me. I love the both of you more than I can ever begin to write and I don't want to leave you, but I really don't want to be around anymore. There are too many people out there who think what I think I am is wrong and, Mom and Dad, I can't be one of those people. Please don't blame yourselves. This is all about me and my choice. I wish there was another way, but I can't think of one. Please don't let anyone else ever read this.

I print out the letter and read it over a few times before getting a pen out my desk and writing, Love, Bradley. I set it down on my bed before walking over and opening the door.

"Mom, I'm really not up for eating. I'm just going to lie down a little longer."

Damn. It's so hard to hide all the pain – all the sadness, especially from her.

"It's okay, Bradley. I'll make up a plate for you and you can just nuke it when you're ready. Are you sure you are okay, hon?"

There's so much concern in her voice.

"Yeah, it's okay, Mom. Honest, I'm just really tired."

"Don't forget to test your blood before you lie down, honey," she says as I hear her walk back into the kitchen.

"Don't worry. I will."

I move quietly to the bathroom and find the extra insulin I always keep upstairs in case I need it during the night. It just makes it easier so I don't have to go downstairs. I take two sleeping pills from the cabinet. You see my dad travels overseas all the time so he has them for the long trips. I head back to my room. I close the door and lock it. Sitting on my bed, I'm overwhelmed with sadness thinking about all the things I'm going to miss. I'll never have the chance to see what college is like or have my first home. But I guess none of that really matters anymore. This is it. Damn, I hate doing this to my parents. I know Sean's death devastated them and losing their only other child will be awful, but I struggle to push those things out of my mind. I'm just too sad and too hurt. I have to do this. God knows, I've thought about it so many times.

I take the two sleeping pills and then fill the syringe all the way with insulin. I know it'll take a while for the insulin to put me into a coma, but the sleeping pills will help ease me into a haze. Slowly I begin to feel my body respond to the tiredness. Suddenly I'm really tired and getting dizzy so I lie down on the bed, carefully placing the letter on my chest. In the distance I can hear the phone ring and my dad's voice. It's getting louder and he sounds angry. Now he's shouting.

"Brad, they're holding Mr. Bobson and, son, we really need to talk. It's okay," he says from outside my door.

Instinctively I try to get out of bed, but I can't. I'm way too dizzy, too weak, too light-headed to do anything like that. My dad's still calling. I can hear him trying to open the door.

"I know it's going to be hard to talk about, Brad, but the police are going to be here in a few minutes and we need to talk before they get here," he pleads as he tries to turn the doorknob.

I hear the door being forced open. My room begins to spin faster and I feel my eyes rolling back in my head. I can hear him calling out from a far distance. It's muffled like I'm wearing headphones or something.

"Brad! It's okay, son. Brad...Brad....Brad. Oh my god! Joan, call 911!"

I don't remember anything else except the entire room going black as my body begins to heave and I know the convulsions have started.

1

"The Play (or movie's) the Thing"

That was almost a year ago. Because my parents arrived when they did, they called 911 and got me to a hospital right away. My dad held onto the note so the paramedics didn't see it. He was afraid it may cause some issues later on. The time spent in the E.R. was a mixed bag to say the least. The crappy part was having to relive the whole Harvey Bobson thing. You see the police came to the hospital to question me. It was so troubling to have to reveal what happened. I had to fill out all these forms and focus my mind of those events when all I wanted was to get well and get out of there and forget Harvey Bobson. Luckily no one seemed to make the connection between me passing out just hours after some creep in his fifties tried to molest me. They seemed to figure that after all I'd had been through, I had just made a mistake with my insulin dose.

Apparently though I was not the first person Harvey had tried to hurt. The police had contacted the families of all of the kids in the pictures. Seems Harvey had listed contact information on the back of the photos which ended up making the investigator's job a whole lot easier. Happily, however, Harvey had never hurt any of those little kids, only guys my age who didn't always come with the security of a parent in tow. In his office they found a list of other high school guys he had "interviewed" and their stories weren't as pretty. I never followed up with what happened to him, probably because I just wanted to get past it, but part of me sure hopes he's still rotting away in jail.

The positive side was that my parents were extremely supportive. They said we'd discuss the letter once we got home but there was nothing to worry about. Of course that's easier said than done. I dreaded the moment when we arrived back at the house and I had finished putting my things away in my room. Soon after, just as I expected, my mom and dad called me down to the family room to talk.

"Brad, you know we love and care about you no matter what. Right?" my dad asked.

"Yeah, of course," I said, registering the pain and exhaustion on my mother's face.

We've always been able to talk easily and so we sat there and talked about why suicide is never the answer, especially for what had happened. I tried to stop them, but they were insistent. They said they understood I was going through a process trying to figure things out, but they'd always continue to support and love me. For some reason I had assumed the conversation would be horrible, but in the end, it was actually what I needed. I still loathe the fact I'm even considering I'm gay, but at least I know my parents are there for me. They did, however, say I needed to see a therapist to talk things out. There was no way I could try and do something as drastic as attempting suicide and not at least have a few conversations with someone who's paid to help. I wanted to fight them on it, but I could see the hope in their eyes, so I agreed.

The sessions weren't all that great really. I told the therapist what I thought she wanted to hear. Talking to a stranger about why I'm having sexual feelings for guys doesn't seem like the right thing for me. If and when I'm ready to talk to someone, it'll be someone I trust and love. No offense to the therapist. She was really nice, but in the end it was best to give her what she needed so I could be allowed to go off to college and get the whole Harvey Bobson thing behind me.

I was extremely lucky to get accepted to Anderson University in Southern California. They have one of the premiere film schools in the country. This was the dream I'd been planning my whole life. However, I still had to convince my parents that it was the best place for me even though it was so far away. They were really concerned about me, but I told them I was past all the crap and there was nothing to worry about. I was really okay and ready for the challenges college would bring. We all flew out to the campus together and they helped get me settled in. They even spoke with the head master of the dorm and explained my diabetes to him. I was a little embarrassed, but I knew this was something they needed to do if I was going to live clear across the country. After all the unpacking was done, I reminded them that I really was okay. They said they understood and my mom gave me a long hug as my dad patted me on the back before they got into the rental car and headed to LAX. I knew they weren't okay with leaving me but they were sure doing a pretty good job of faking it. I just wish I was half as happy and secure as I had just told them I was.

Now here I am eight months later sitting on my side of a dorm room I share with a roommate who has a web cam on his computer where he does kinky things with his girlfriend four states away. I've been trying to mind my own business, but the guy is gross. So here I go again, putting on my headphones as I try to read over my survey of Western Civ notes before falling asleep.

I've got to get some sleep tonight because I have a big day ahead of me tomorrow. Not only do I have a Western Civ exam that's going to be hell on earth, but I also have a date with Mary. I know my therapist told me I needed to try and explore the life that comes with being gay, but it ain't happening yet. To make my friends happy (and keep them off my back) I go out on dates with girls. I guess deep down, I also hope there's still a chance with the ladies. Most of the dates I've gone on haven't been the greatest, but I think there might just be something with Mary as we met under the strangest of circumstances.

You see Mary and I met on a student film set. I had volunteered to act in a short film for a friend of mine. It was pretty easy stuff. The director told me all I had to do was walk in front of the camera and blow a girl a kiss. That was it. Once the shot was finished, I figured I'd go back to my dorm room and hang for a bit. Then he turns to me and says, "Okay, it's time for the sex scene." Having just taken a slug of Diet Coke, I did a note-worthy Danny Thomas spit take. Recovering, I asked what the hell he was talking about. He explained that the guy whose part I was playing had dropped out and he'd had to rework the script. Great, a struggling guy with gay tendencies gets to do a simulated sex scene with a complete stranger who happens to be of the female persuasion. What are the odds? Regardless, I had committed to doing it and I was actually starting to become a little comfortable around Mary (We'd only met today, but we had chatted a little before the production started) so maybe I could pull this off. My only problem was I was afraid our relatively new friendship would fizzle once she saw me with my shirt off. I'm not in bad shape but I'm not exactly Hugh Jackman either and all I needed was for the movie to turn into a horror film or laugh fest.

Before they began filming, it had been nice chatting with Mary. We immediately seemed to hit it off. We had a lot of things in common and liked most of the same movies. She's very cute. Has short brunette hair and wonderful blue eyes. Once we got on set though, the tension started. There were lights everywhere and it was extremely hot. The director, Andy, a nice enough guy who was a year ahead of me, told us to get into bed, take our shirts off, and we'd go from there. Outside of my encounter with Harvey Bobson, I don't think I was ever as scared as I was right then.

Mary put her hand on my shoulder and said, "Listen, it's gonna be fine. I'm sure it's not going to take that long and we sort of know each other, right?"

"Um, sure," I replied nervously.

"Then don't worry about it, Brad. It'll be fun. I promise to be gentle," she said with an accompanying coy wink.

As bluntly as any director could, Andy asked us to get under the covers and start rolling around. Okay, before I go any further let me set the scene for you. I'm playing the guy that's having sex with the main character's girlfriend, a.k.a. Mary. As we are "doing it" the boyfriend walks into the room, sees us and storms out. Pretty easy scene, made even easier since the beauty of this assignment was there was no audio so at least I wasn't going to be expected to make any convincing noises.

As we got under the covers, Andy yelled "cut" and said there's no way the camera was going to be able to show what's really going on. In the back of my head, I can hear him telling me I need to get on top of her and start thrusting.

"Um, what?" I asked with a lot less confidence in my voice than I wish I had.

"Come on, Brad…you've done this before. Just get on top of Mary and thrust your hips forward like you're fucking her for a few seconds and we'll be good," Andy explained with the exasperation of a far more seasoned director. "No offense, Mary," he added finally taking his eyes away from me.

"None taken," Mary replied laughing then looked at me seductively and whispered, "Oh, baby!"

I felt like that guy in *Sex and the City* (yes, I like that show) who thinks he knows where the clitoris is and Samantha has to keep telling him it's a little to the left. Hell, you could draw one for me and have Siri give me directions and I'd still be fumbling. I mean I've never done anything remotely like this in my life.

Mary said she was ready and fine with Andy's directives and I felt about as reassured as Han Solo as they were lowering him into the frozen carbonite. I only hoped I was putting on as good an act as he did. Andy was as focused as I'd ever seen him and he seemed to be in a rush the entire time. Between the pressure and the hot lights, I was sweating like a pig and probably even looking like I'd been having some pretty intense sex.

A few very uncomfortable thrusts later, Andy yelled "Cut" and that was it. Suddenly I was putting my shirt back on and walking out of my first and hopefully last simulated sex scene. As I was leaving, Mary asked if she could walk back to the dorm with me as we both lived in Melrose, a high rise on the opposite end of campus.

"So, I guess there's a first time for everything right," she said with a smirk on her face.

"What do ya mean?" I questioned as I felt my sweat glands going into high gear once again. Maybe I should consider buying stock in a major deodorant company.

"Having fake sex on camera, silly," she said laughing.

Trying to seem cavalier, I commented that it probably didn't faze her since low budget porn movies were how she was paying her way through college. She reached out with her left hand and punched my upper arm jokingly. We continued to chat on the walk across campus when I suddenly realized I was becoming more and more comfortable with her. Maybe, just maybe, this was the step in the direction I was looking for. No more of this gay stuff. It was time for the ladies – or at least I hoped so.

As we reached the dorm, I sorted blurted out whether she'd be interested in going bowling with me tomorrow afternoon, just the two of us.

"Yeah, that'd be great," she said. "How about around 3:00ish?"

I was so excited I think I said something like of course that would be great I will see you then. She laughed knowing how nervous I was and smiled saying something like she couldn't wait for some non-sex time with me.

Unlocking the door to my room, I couldn't believe what I'd just done. I can't think of any date I've been on that hasn't made me really uncomfortable and I'm so afraid this one will be no exception. But, somehow it seems there is something there with Mary that just might change everything.

2

"Friendship is constant in all other things"

When I get back to my room my two best friends are waiting outside the door for me. Chris, my best friend from high school, also decided to join me at Anderson. He's studying Business and Economics and Anderson is rated highly for that as well. It's good for me to have a familiar face around (even though that face still sometimes appears in my dreams). Chris has always been there for me. When I ended up in the hospital that last semester of high school, he brought me my homework every day. He claimed he wasn't really being a friend, because only an asshole would bring his best friend all his homework. I have a feeling he asked my parents what happened with my internship because he never brought it up even when I ended up working at the local drug store for the entire summer. The hardest part with Chris is there are still those moments when

I look at him and I sometimes imagine what a life would be like with him. He's just so good looking. He's a little taller than me and has these amazing broad shoulders. But in the end it's his big brown eyes that really lure you in. But right now, I need to block those thoughts out and focus on Mary.

Then there is my other best friend, Laura. She and I are pretty much like the proverbial two peas in a pod. She's always there for me not only to express the feminine point of view, but also to be the shoulder to lean on when anything might go wrong. The funny thing is I think she would be the first person I would talk to about all this gay stuff. We actually dated for a short time first semester, but like all of my dates, it didn't really go anywhere. We decided maybe we were meant to be best friends and not a couple. I'm sure when I asked for a hug on the third date, as opposed to a kiss or much more for that matter, that was saying something. However, I think it was a good decision for both of us. I wish I could tell the both Laura and Chris all the crap in my head, but for now it needs to stay where it is, locked away.

"So, how did the filming go, buddy?" Chris asks immediately.

Laughingly I explain a little of the shoot, but say in the end he was just going to have to wait for the premiere on campus. Laura pounces on me with a multitude of questions mostly about what it was like hanging out with Mary for the day.

"It was cool, I guess. I mean she's fun. Actually I asked her out tomorrow to go bowling," I reply with a small smile.

"And…?" they both ask at the same time.

"And, of course she said yes," I say with that smirk I love to give when I have done something pretty impressive.

"Holy shit...you are the man!" screams Chris.

The both of them could not stop talking for the next ten minutes as we walk over to the cafeteria for dinner. The questions range from how I got the balls to ask her out to how am I going to prepare for the date.

"Uh, prepare? I figured I'd get dressed and then go get her and that would be it," I say rather shocked by the question.

"Please...ugh this is going to take all dinner to get you ready for tomorrow," Laura says with a huge sigh. "Mary is awesome and we need to make sure you are at your charming best," Laura explains.

For the next forty minutes, I'm bombarded with question after question, while trying to eat cafeteria meat loaf that tastes nothing like the kind my mom makes. All the things they think I should ask her and then all the stuff I should expect she is going to ask me. I try to explain to them that we're just going bowling and this isn't speed dating. This doesn't seem to win them over, however. After dinner I tell them I need to do a little reading and get to bed early. Before they leave though, Laura comes over to me and gave me a big hug.

"You deserve this, Brad. You're a great guy that deserves an amazing date with a wonderful girl like Mary. Have fun. This is good," she says in the most caring voice I've ever heard her use.

So here I am, lying in bed, getting ready to take another plunge into the somewhat unknown world of dating. Now let me get something straight first. As I explained to Laura, this is far from the first date I've ever been on. I went out on a bunch of dates in high school and even a few first semester, Laura included. I just never seemed to make a real connection with any of them. I don't think it had everything to do with the gay thing. I just don't seem to have the confidence that's needed in the dating scene. It always seemed like the other guys at school had no problem just going up to girls and asking them out. I'm sure that's not how it always went with them and maybe they got just as many rejections as the next guy. But I know it's just harder for me. Life just seems to be harder for me.

But this is the time when things are going to change. I'm going to go out with Mary tomorrow night and it's going to go amazingly well. We're going to have the greatest time and I'm going to win her over and take her back to my dorm and we'll….Okay, I highly doubt we'll be going back to the dorm and doing anything, especially with my strange roommate who seems to be awake at all hours.

After a quick shower and getting into my boxers and tee shirt, I decide to search the net a little before bed. I start searching for things like: How to have the perfect date and things you should and shouldn't do on a first date. Everything said on one site seemed to contradict the next one. Finally its time to call it quits. Tomorrow's going to be the day I set myself on the path of finally dating a girl long term. All I need to do is suppress these gay thoughts and feelings and I'm set. I can do this. I can do this. Can I really do this? I sigh as I set the alarm.

3

"All is the fear and nothing is the love"

This is it. God, that's so cliché, but it really feels like this is my last chance to make it with a girl. Mary's great and I think she could be the one to turn this around for me. Problem is when I was doing the scene with her, I didn't feel anything sexual. Was I supposed to? I mean of all situations I've been in that should have been the one to cause some stirring, right? I'm sure some people would say with all those people around I might not get aroused, but I can't stop the nagging in the back of my head that just seems to be another indicator saying it just isn't meant to be. I also don't want to over think this. I tend to do that way too much. I just want to have a good time tonight.

What really matters is that we have fun – right? I have to stop expecting everything to fall into place all at once. Gotta keep my expectations in check.

Okay, so here I am, standing in the hallway of her dorm ringing my hands as usual. Go on. Knock on the door, you idiot.

"Hey, Brad. You look cute. I'm all ready to go. You want me to drive or do you?" she asks with a smile that shows off her amazingly white teeth (something I've always appreciated). She's wearing a really cute *Life is Good* blue tee shirt with a smiley girl riding a bike.

"Um, yeah, you look cute too...nice shirt. Sure, I can drive," I say.

Try to be smooth, kid, I tell myself as my mind shifts into high gear with all the self-coaching.

"Great, let's do this thing. I hope you aren't afraid of losing to a girl though," she says with a taunting tone that I know is her playful attempt to relax me.

I smile back at her, actually starting to relax a little. Driving to the bowling alley, I'm anything but creative as I start to make small talk asking what classes she likes and what she wants to do after college. It's pretty easy stuff and I'm starting to feel more and more comfortable. I even bring up the fact that the shirt she's wearing was probably designed somewhere near my hometown because that's where *Life is Good* is based. Now that's a bit of cocktail information I'm actually proud of.

It takes about 20 minutes or so to get to the bowling alley. It's never about distance in Los Angeles; it's always all about the traffic. Finally we exit the 101 and pull into the lot of a bowling alley on Ventura Blvd. While I look for a place to park, I make the decision that it'll be best if I pay for everything. That's what guys do, right?

"By the way, Mary, just letting you know upfront I'll be paying for everything tonight so no need to reach into that gigantic purse you're carrying," I say with a smile.

"I thought that'd ease any tension at the end of the night," I say with some confidence, knowing there'd still be that tension of should I kiss her or not at the end of the date.

"Well that is very sweet of you, Brad," she says as we leave the car and I set the alarm.

Walking into the building, she slips her arm through mine and says far too seriously, "You know, Brad, I was a little nervous about going out on this date."

"What's there to be nervous about?" I mumble, my words catching in my throat. This is probably not a good thing.

"Well, this is the first time I've had a date with someone *after* having sex with them," she giggles.

Hoping my relief isn't as obvious as I'm feeling, I try for a quick comeback.

"Really? So nothing's really come from working the streets all this time?"

Mary leans over and lightly punches me on the shoulder. As she hits me, her foot slips on some spilt soda on the floor. I catch her before she bites it completely. Suddenly her face is inches away from mine. She starts to close her eyes in anticipation of a kiss. I lift her to her feet and give her a hug.

"You okay?" I ask.

"Yeah, yeah, I'm okay. I'm good," she says pushing back her hair.

"I'll talk to the manager about the wet floor. You want some nachos," I ask. I know, I know, really smooth. I'm just not ready for this kiss. Hell, we didn't even kiss during the film shoot. The problem is I can tell she's embarrassed. Actually, I think she's a little hurt by my seeming rejection.

Damn, I have to defuse this.

"Sorry. I…just…um."

Turning back to me, Mary smiles and pulls off a perfect recovery. "It's okay, Brad. There's no need to rush into anything. In fact it was kind of chivalrous of you not to make the moves on me when I was in such a vulnerable position. Well it's out, I guess," she says with a smile. "It's probably better you know I'm not the most graceful person before I pick up the ball."

Damn, she's got such a cute smile, I think, as we walk over to the counter and get our shoes before finally finding the bowling balls that fit our fingers and are the right weight.

As we start bowling I finally realize I'm even relaxing my shoulders a little bit. Each time she gets a strike I give her a high five or a hug.

After four games we're pretty much bowled out. Despite all her claims of being clumsy, she beats me two out of the first three games. The last game is pretty close though, 117 to 109, so I don't feel too bad beating her.

"So, killer, you want to go back to my place and watch a movie or something?" I ask.

Mary seems quick to reply with a yes. God, I hope my roommate's gone.

After glancing through my wide array of movies, let's face it, I have everything from *Singin' in the Rain* to *True Lies*, she smiles and pulls out *When Harry Met Sally.*

"I figured since we faked it the other day and Meg Ryan's so good at faking her orgasms that it's a perfect fit," she says with a laugh and a look that should be getting some response out of me, but I still don't feel it.

About half way through the movie, I decide to cut to the chase. Lifting my arm, I put it around her shoulders. She makes a pleasant little sound of contentment and rests her head on my shoulder.

"You know I've been waiting for you to do that," she whispers.

Thank god I've done something right. Slowly I begin stroking the back of her hair and neck and even get the courage to blow in her ear. She has incredibly soft hair and smooth skin, kind of like silk.

"Oh, that feels really good, Brad. Do you mind rubbing my shoulders?"

"Sure." I begin to lightly rub her shoulders hoping that this will illicit a sexual response from both of us. But let's be honest, I'm more worried about my reaction than hers at this point.

"Oh, that feels so good. You know you can massage me in other places if you want," she says in a quiet voice.

Confidently, she guides my hands to her breasts, which seem bigger than I thought. This still doesn't seem to be turning me on and I know it should. She slowly moves my hands underneath her shirt and then lets go of my hands and starts undoing her bra herself, and I'm just thinking "Thank god". She once more reaches for my hands and places them on her breasts. She turns her head and I begin to kiss her on the lips.

Somehow I figure there would be some sort of spark when we kiss, but it just feels so mechanical, not passionate at all. Then she does the one thing I hope she wouldn't. She reaches down to my crotch and find there to be very little physical reaction on my part. She continues rubbing for a while longer and then moves her hand away.

I immediately move backwards and apologize saying I have no idea what's going on, quickly telling her she's hot, and maybe this all has to do with my blood sugar – thank you, Harvey Bobson!

"It's okay, Brad. I should probably go home anyway. I didn't realize it was so late and I've really got a lot to do tomorrow."

"Please, Mary, I'm sorry."

"Come on, Brad; it's cool. I promise we'll finish this up another time."

After hooking her bra, Mary leans over and kisses me on the lips and says something that hits me as really weird.

"Don't ever be afraid of who you are," she whispers and then leaves the room.

Since my roommate is gone for the evening, I have the room to myself and right about now that's good. I walk over to my desk and sit. Turning my chair to face the wall, I punch it really hard. Pretty stupid 'cause my hand starts to bleed all over the place and doesn't begin to address my problem, but I figure if I'm alone, I'm allowed to be pissed. After controlling myself a little, I decide that what happened tonight really is the proof I need to explore my gay side. After washing my hand in the sink and putting on a few band-aids,

I come back to my desk and face the empty computer screen. I go to Yahoo search and type in "hot gay guy pics". Over one million links appear on the screen. Shit. Let's face it. This isn't the first time I've looked on the internet for this stuff, but in the end I always convinced myself to look at the straight porn, knowing that even then my eyes were never really looking at the girls.

Frustrated with everything, I click on the X and shut down the computer. My god damn gay journey can start tomorrow. Right now I want the darkness only sleep can provide. Ready for bed, I run tonight's date through my mind one more time to see if there was something I could have done differently. Although I've been thinking about this gay thing for a long time, this is really the first time I know I need to do something about it. Reality check, kid, it's time to face facts. Closing my eyes, I wrap the pillow around my face and cry uncontrollably until I can't cry anymore. It can't be so bad to be gay; right? I keep saying this in my head until sleep finally arrives.

Suddenly I'm standing in the middle of the auditorium at my high school. It's graduation day and I'm looking not too shabby with my white button-down shirt and blue rep tie underneath my gown. I'm excited and proud. I've worked really hard for this. Graduating with honors in high school is pretty cool.

They're announcing the graduates' names and per the usual, I begin running my hands through my legs. Finally after the person sitting next to me is called, I hear my name.

"Bradley Archer", the school principal calls.

"Way to go, faggot," I hear someone yell, but there's no way someone would do that here – not at a graduation ceremony. I must have just heard it wrong.

The walk to the podium is a long one and as I look around I notice there are disgusted looks on the faces of many of the people as I walk by. What the hell's going on?

Finally I reach the podium and Principal Roskins hands me my diploma.

Whispering in my ear as he shakes my hand, he says, "Well done, pussy boy."

"What!" I reply completely astonished at his remark. Then he turns around and there is a flash of a camera that freezes this moment in time.

Returning to my seat, I pass by dozens of my classmates and they're all muttering under their breath words like faggot, pussy, cocksucker, sissy, bottom boy.

I close my eyes trying to wish this all away. There's no way people know I'm gay. And even if they do, they'd never react like this.

Suddenly I feel a hand on my shoulder. It's one of my friends from drama club, Mitch.

"Don't worry, Brad. It's no big deal. I just have one question though?" he asks seeming genuinely concerned.

Hoping this is the end of this and people will just move on I reply, "Um, sure?"

"Does it hurt when you get ass fucked by another guy, faggot?"

"What the hell are you talking about? I thought you were my friend?"

"I was your friend until I learned that you like to bend over for other guys. I mean that's sick, man. God, your parents must be so embarrassed."

"Hey, fuck you, man! My parents love me no matter what. And I'm not gay, so piss off," I retort as I move to my seat.

"Yeah, sure whatever, butt boy. Just stay the hell away from me."

I turn around to see my parents, who are sitting a few rows behind me. They look at me with disappointment in their eyes and start to walk out of the auditorium.

This can't be happening. I mean seriously– this can't be happening. Suddenly there's a swarm of my fellow students surrounding me – all pointing, pointing at me.

Faggot! Faggot! Faggot! They keep yelling with their accusatory fingers jabbing at my face. I start to cry.

"Aw, is the little faggot sad 'cause he's being called out on what he is? *You* are an abomination," one of them screams.

"You're gonna burn in hell," screams another.

I close my eyes as tightly as I can and cover my ears. This needs to stop. This needs to go away.

NO! NO! NO!

"NO!"

"Wake up, man," my roommate Jonathan says shaking my shoulders. After a few moments, I pull myself together, apologize to my roommate and ask if I was talking in my sleep.

"Naw. You were just screaming out "No" over and over. Not that really I care, but are you all right, Brad?"

"Yeah, Yeah, I'm fine. Sorry about that."

"Jesus, you scared the shit outta me. How about giving a guy a night of undisturbed rest," he says as he pulls his sheet over his head.

"Yeah, sorry. I'll give it a try."

Getting out of bed, I notice I've sweated through my tee shirt and boxer shorts. I go over to the dresser and grab replacements and head to the bathroom, closing the door behind me. Turning on the shower, I take off my shirt and boxers and step in, letting the water envelop me. After only a few seconds, I start crying again. Sinking to the floor I put my face in my hands. I can't stop crying. Why can't I be like everyone else? Why does life have to be so damn difficult for me? Not only do I have this fucking diabetes that is never out of my mind for more than a few minutes, but I also have this god damn gay thing. I don't even know what the hell to call it.

What if my dream is right and everyone already knows I'm gay?

What if people really do react like that and decide they don't want any part of me? That they never want to be in my life?

No, no that could never happen. We're way past all of that. People don't judge like that anymore. But, how do I know what people are really feeling? What if deep down my parents really do hate me? This whole thing could leave me completely alone.

I step out of the shower and dry off. I move over to the sink and open the medicine cabinet. There are so many little amber plastic vials filled with pills – pills for headaches and other prescriptions for my roommate. Opening the caps, I dump out about two dozen pills into my hand—brightly colored pills that actually look harmless. No more nightmares, no more anxiety, no more Harvey Bobson, no more nothing. I can finally rest.

Just as I open my mouth to toss in the entire handful, I see my mother crying over my bed when I tried this last time. Very slowly I take the pills and put them back in their respective bottles. This isn't the answer and I know it. I close the bathroom door behind me as quietly as possible – the last thing I need now is Jonathan waking up and asking me if I'm okay.

Moving to the computer, I type in the words "gay anonymous suicide hotline". A link to a website appears. This seems to be the right place for me to call. It's literally a hotline for suicidal teens questioning their sexuality. I know I don't really want to kill myself but I just need to get some of this out. I just need to talk to someone who might begin to understand.

Scribbling down the number on a piece of paper, I change into jeans and a tee shirt and grab my keys and the paper with the number on it. I quickly shove it in my pocket and leave the room as quietly as I can. As I walk around campus, the tension of making the call is killing me. Finally, I find a more secluded area (everywhere is pretty secluded at two in the morning) with a bench under a street light. Pulling out my phone, I start dialing the number.

As the ringing continues, I figure it must be too late and go to press the END button, when a female voice answers.

"Help hotline."

I take a deep breath and say, "Um, yes, my name is… Joe and I really need to talk to someone."

"Hi, Joe. My name is Clair. We can talk about anything you want this evening. Do you mind if I ask how you're feeling right now?"

"Yeah, sure. I'm not suicidal if that is what you're trying to find out. I did something really stupid a little while ago and now I just need to let it out."

"Okay, sure. This thing you did, Joe, can you talk about it? Are you sure you're okay?

"Yeah, I almost took some pills, but I put them all back. Don't worry I didn't take any of them," I say trying desperately to explain myself to this complete stranger.

"Well that's certainly good to hear. Please remember, Joe, that you only tell me the things you're comfortable sharing. Everything you choose to share with me is strictly confidential, okay?"

For the next hour or so I spill my guts out to a person I don't know that probably lives on the other side of the country. I know I said earlier that I wouldn't tell a stranger the things I'm going through, but after tonight I don't think I have much of a choice. Clair was incredibly nice on the phone. She just seemed so sincere telling me that she could help show me how to go about exploring the possibility of being gay and that it really is okay.

I even tell her all about Harvey Bobson and the dreams I've been having. Finally after I finish, she asks what college I go to. I figure after telling her all of this it couldn't hurt to let her know where I go to school.

"Anderson University, in L.A.," I say in a more relaxed tone.

"Okay, thanks, Joe. Do you know there's an organization on campus that works with people who might be having the same issues you are? Maybe that would be a place where you can go to meet some people you can talk to face to face," she continues.

"You do know, Joe, that you're not going to be able to just will this thing away right?"

"Yeah, I know. I'm not totally sure why I'm even feeling this way. Maybe tomorrow I'll give this center you're talking about a chance."

Clair continues to give me some specifics about this group and where I can find them on campus. She says that if I want, we can talk some more.

"No. I'm feeling much better now, but I'm really tired. Thank you, Clair. I'm gonna check out the LGBT Center. Honest," I say.

I hope she realizes how sincere my thank you is as we end the call.

Heading back to my room, I feel an intense gripping in my stomach. It's an ache that I've felt for a long time, but it's worse now than ever before. The fear of confronting this elephant in the room of my life is so intense I want to vomit. I take some very deep breaths as I slide my card through the slot and enter my room.

Crawling into bed, I shut my eyes and begin to imagine all these different memories that have nothing to do with this struggle. Things like my last birthday, or the day I met one of my best friends, Laura, memories – good memories, or that time in high school at the State Drama Festival when I got a standing ovation. I wrap myself in these memories –good memories– as I drift into sleep hoping the anxiety won't return until morning when I plan to confront it face on.

4

"I stand in pause where I shall first begin, And both neglect"

Waking up the next morning, I wonder if yesterday and last night were all part of a nightmare. Glancing over to my desk, it's still there, now a crumpled piece of paper with the phone number for the hotline that I put there when I got home. After a few seconds of panic, I calm myself by breathing in slowly and try and recall everything that was positive from the call last night. I mean, she helped me. I gotta remember that. It's time to start this journey. Seeing that my roommate has already left for the morning, I get up, go over and sit in front of my computer and once again start the search.

Taking a moment, I breathe in deeply trying to relax my tense shoulders. I look down at my hand and give it a little rub. The pain's not too bad considering how hard I hit the wall last night. After a silent pep talk, I close my eyes and try to imagine what I want to see. In the Google search box, I start typing "college gay guys". Thousands of links pop up. I click on the first link and the main page is filled with naked guys around my age. Even with the fact that much of this is new to me, I have to admit that I've gone to a few of the sites listed on the page. Every time I went to these pages before I would get sick to my stomach and close the site. However, this time I decide to take my time and explore one of the websites as well as few others. Finally I feel a stirring in my crotch, but what surprises me most is the picture that elicits the most reaction is the one that looks like Chris. Christ, he's never going to be out of my mind. Damn, why do I feel a so dirty doing this? Do people really look at porn all the time?

Unable to move to the next step, I get up and start to pace, ringing my hands nervously. Finally, I pick up the university guide directory and thumb through it looking for the student activities section. There it is. Just what I'm looking for, the LGBT club on campus known as "OutAnderson". It looks like much more than just a club though. The description says it helps people who are struggling with their sexuality or gender identity.

I jot down the location of the club in the back of my notebook, pick up my bag, turn off the monitor, give myself a quick check in the mirror, raise my hand to my mouth to check my breath, and slowly close the door behind me.

My film studies class isn't for two hours so I have plenty of time. Walking over to the student activities building feels like a twenty mile hike. I'm so enwrapped with everything that's gone on in the past 24 hours that I don't realize Chris walking right beside me.

"Yo. What's up? So…how was your date last night?" Chris says smiling. "I figure since you didn't call it went well."

"Yeah. We had fun," I answer sort of matter of factly.

"We had fun?" That's it? Come on! I tell you all about my dates. Give me a break; let me live vicariously through you just this one time, man."

Hesitating, I finally say, "Well, let's just say her tits are even nicer to touch than to look at." God, I feel like such a dick saying something like that. That's just not me.

"That's slightly crass for you, buddy, but second base on the first date? Not too shabby, my friend," he says giving me a fist bump and I return the favor.

My mind begins to wander for a second and I look away. As I turn back to him, I'm seeing the body of the guy on the internet with Chris's head, and he's naked! Great! While I'm inadvertently thinking of him naked, Chris is randomly talking about his chemistry final!

Feeling wicked uncomfortable, I quickly shake my head and tell him I've gotta run.

"Um, okay cool. You wanna meet up for lunch later?" he asks.

"Yeah, yeah. Sounds good. Gotta go," I reply trying to sound like nothing's bothering me. Right!

"Hey, Brad, you all right?"

"I'm good. I just realized I've got to print out something for my next class or I'm screwed."

"All right, cool. Lunch around one?" he questions.

"Yeah, sure - great - see ya at one," I say but as I turn to head off I see him shaking his head.

God dammit, I hate lying, especially to him.

As soon as I enter the building, I make a beeline for the restrooms. Thank god there's no one in here. I head to a stall, close the door, and begin to dry heave. My stomach had a hard enough time looking at gay porn, but imagining my best friend naked is crazy.

After taking a few deep breaths, I calm myself enough to head to the place I know I need to be. Walking up the staircase, my hands start shaking again. If I do this, if I walk into that room, than I'm admitting to myself and ultimately to the world that I'm gay. I have no idea who's going to be in there; there could easily be someone I know from my classes or the dorm. Once they see me, that'll be it. I'll be out for the rest of my life. Closing my eyes, I assure myself I can do this, but as I get to the entrance, I just can't. I find a small table and take a seat across the way so I can watch people walking in and out. Finally, I walk over and open the door and walk through.

So this is it, the LGBT Center. There are a few computers in the main room and a conference table in the middle. On the outside wall there are four offices. Some of the doors are closed. People are everywhere. There are one on one conversations happening, people with concerned faces talking quietly on the phones, and even some people in the back corner watching a movie. I think it's *Prayers for Bobby* with Sigourney Weaver. Some people are crying quietly as they watch. An older gentleman, maybe in his mid-fifties, starts walking over to me. As quickly as we make eye contact, I turn around and start walking away, but he puts his hand on my shoulder, my shoulder which is so tense I'm sure I'm gonna to feel it tomorrow.

"Hey, there. I'm George. I'm one of the advisers here at the Center," he says and I immediately notice his eyes have a kindness and concern that I haven't seen since I left home and a smile that truly seems welcoming.

"I figured I should introduce myself before you leave," he continues with a reassuring voice.

I have absolutely no idea what to say to this man. I'm not even sure if I can say anything. After a few moments, only because I can't stand the silence, I introduce myself.

"Um, yeah, my name's Josh," I stammer. "I was just passing by, but I think I'm in the wrong place. Sorry to bother you."

"Please, it's no bother, Josh, but are you really sure you're in the wrong place?" he questions.

There's such concern on his face that I want to just open up and say everything. But, as I'm about to, the image of Harvey Bobson's face floats before me and I can't do it.

"Sorry, I don't think I'm quite ready for this," I say with anxiety that I'm pretty sure is blaring across my face.

"I understand. This is probably a hard time you're going through right now. Well, look, Josh, here's my number at the Center. I check my voicemail all the time so if it's an emergency, I'll get back to you quickly and remember you can always come here. The hours are printed on my card. This is a safe place, Josh, and there really are a lot of great people you can talk to."

I take his card and shake his hand. There's some comfort in the firmness, but I just can't seem to say what I feel.

After my film class, which I don't think I paid all that much attention to, I walk back to the dorm. About half way there, I stop for a moment. One of the great things about this school is the campus grounds. The school does an amazing job at keeping it incredibly clean and the lawns are always green even though it never seems to rain in Los Angeles. They have this area where people can throw a Frisbee around or just lie in the sun. I come here a lot, but usually with friends. Finding a rather large tree away from most of the people, I sit, leaning my back against its trunk. I'm so pissed off at myself. All I feel is that the strength I know I've always had as a person is drifting away as I continue to move deeper and deeper into both the closet and depression. I seem to be taking baby steps forward and then giant leaps backwards. The thing is I really want to be free. It's quiet out here and I'm physically and mentally exhausted so I close my eyes.

Suddenly I'm in the car again with Harvey Bobson, but this time I'm less scared than I've been before. I've had this dream dozens and dozens of times and this is the first time I don't panic when Harvey begins to talk to me explaining how good he is going to make me feel. Instead of looking away, I stare at him, trying to burn his eyes with my fierce look.

"I hate you," I scream. "You're one of the reasons why after all this time I'm still in the fucking closet. I hate myself because of you. You took away any innocence I had. You made me afraid of gay people and afraid of myself. All I've been looking for since I met you is how not to be gay. How not to be myself. You made me find all the things that are wrong with being gay, and damn it all, I hate you for that. You're a despicable human being and I'm done with this. I'm no longer going to be afraid. I will no longer allow you to have control over me. I am not you and never will be. I'm going to be okay and I'm going to get through this. Got it, pervert!"

There's defeat on Harvey's face as he gets out of his car and walks into the darkness until I can't see him anymore. Suddenly, I wake up. There are tears running down my cheeks. After wiping my face with my sleeve, I quickly get up from the lawn and head back toward the dorm. Since there's no one around, I sneak into an alley between two of the buildings where I know there won't be anyone. Facing the wall, I start to kick it. For the first time since Harvey Bobson attacked me, I cry openly. I sob like I never have in my life. I'm bawling and then I let out a primal scream. I don't care if anyone hears me! I need this! I don't try to stop the flow of tears. I need a release.

After a few minutes I begin to find my composure. I'm going to be a happy person and the only way I can truly do that is to grow some balls and take some god damn control.

Walking back to the dorm, I go right instead of turning left to go into the building. I just keep on walking. Without even thinking, before I know it, I'm in front of the LGBT Center. Figuring the office is closed, I start to walk away. But there's a light on in one of the end rooms. Looking through the glass, I see George sitting there working on his computer. With no hesitation this time, I knock on the door and wait.

"George?" I ask tentatively.

"Oh, it's Josh, right?" he says with a smile.

"Um, you know, um if you have a moment, I actually think I'm in the right place," I stammer awkwardly.

"I'm glad to hear that, Josh. I'm just finishing up here. Why don't we get a cup of coffee and we can talk for a little bit. Is that all right?"

"After all I've been going through, I think I'd love to have a cup of coffee," I say with more happiness than I've felt in a long time.

"Sounds good, Josh I'm glad you came back."

"It's time for me to be honest with myself. I don't wanna to be sad anymore about who I am," I say finally believing I'm ready to face this.

"And there's no reason to be, Josh. You are who you are and that's cool. I know it sort of sounds like a Hallmark card, but it's true," he says as he shuts his laptop and puts it in his briefcase and places his free hand on my shoulder.

"Some time soon you're going to feel a weight lifted from your chest and shoulders, Josh. You're about to start the next journey in your life and it is going to be awesome because you're finally going to allow yourself to be you. Do you think you're ready for that?" he asks.

"Yeah, I'm ready," I answer.

"Good. Then let's get started," he says as he looks and then closes the door behind us.

5

"O this learning, what a thing it is!"

Setting our coffees on the table, the waitress turns and walks towards the kitchen. George reaches over and takes a few Splendas from the wire caddie between us and starts talking.

"Josh, when I was a kid it was harder, a lot harder to come out of the closet. Don't get me wrong. I'm not saying your experience isn't tough. I just mean, for starters, I grew up in a really small conservative town in the South and people there most certainly didn't talk about homosexuality. In fact, no matter where you lived, people just didn't talk about being gay. By the way, Josh, this was the early seventies if you're wondering how old I am," he says with a chuckle in his voice.

"It was all very under the radar. There weren't any gay bars, certainly not where I was living, and there was no real way to meet other gay men," he says almost matter of factly.

"If there weren't any bars or other gay people out, how could you begin to figure out if you were gay?" I ask with concern and curiosity.

"Well, I'm guessing it was pretty much the same as it is with you. Deep down I just knew. There was nothing on TV back then or in the movies and forget the nightly news. It wasn't until I was around your age, when I was in college in New York, that I had the chance to finally meet some people who were like me. Even in the big city though there weren't many gay bars, but I found a few. The problem was there were raids back then," he says as a serious look clouds his face.

"What do you mean raids?" I ask conjuring up visuals of club carrying cops going into dark basement lounges during the Prohibition.

"Josh, have you ever heard of Stonewall before?"

"No, is it a section of New York?" I ask having no idea what he's talking about.

"Ah, to be young," George says as he leans back into the vinyl booth.

"In many places at that time sodomy was illegal and although going to a gay bar was not actually against the law, they were still raided by the police and people were routinely arrested. Getting arrested was sort of like being blackballed. The local highly respected doctor, salesman, lawyer – he could have been in the crowd that night and his name or picture could have easily made the next morning's newspaper. Once you were outed, it could be next to impossible to find employment. Finally during one of the raids, the men fought back and a riot broke out. This was in 1969. Many men were arrested, but this time it made the national news and that changed things. The world was finally learning about us. Although the gay civil rights movement had been going on for years before, Josh, especially in Los Angeles, most gays believe the Stonewall riots were the kick start to all the pride and civil rights groups we have today."

"God, I had absolutely no idea, George. I knew it must have been rough for people back then, but I had no idea you could be arrested simply for being gay."

"I know it's hard to believe, Josh, but a lot of good has happened in the last 40 years," he says with hope in his eyes.

"But if everything's so good now, George, then why the hell is it so difficult for me to accept it?" I ask still baffled by my own situation.

"Just because life is easier for gay people today doesn't mean there still isn't a whole lot of homophobia in this world, Josh. Just from the time we've spent talking here tonight, I think you're dealing with it mostly internally. I think you know that most of your friends and your family are going to be okay with you being gay. You just can't seem to get over the fact yourself. Am I right?" he asks.

"Yeah, I guess that's it, George. So what am I gonna do? I'm so god damn angry all the time. I literally think about it constantly. I've gotta get past this or I'm seriously gonna go crazy," I say with frustration, anger, and sadness.

"You have to remember, Josh, that this is your journey and no one else's. The decision and the path you follow is going to be yours, all yours. I can help guide you a little bit, but I can't force you to confront it. Why not come by the office a few times this week and I'll introduce you to some of the guys and girls at the Center. Maybe you can make some friends and they can show you what it's like to be a young gay person," he says with a reassuring smile.

"Meeting people your own age will be a good thing. I'm sure many of them have stories similar to yours and they'll tell you how they got through it."

"I guess I can stop by. I just really need to concentrate on my studies too. I mean I can't fall behind. I have to start working on my first short film in the next few weeks and I have no idea what I'm gonna do," I say wondering if I'm really just dodging his invite to meet other gay students on campus.

Once again, George puts his hand on my shoulder, smiles and tells me to take it one step at a time reassuring me that there really is no reason to rush into anything.

"There is more to life, Josh, then being gay and it's important to remember that too," he says as we get up from the booth.

Leaving the coffee shop, we walk to his car. The coffee shop is near campus so I can walk back to my dorm from here. As he reaches for the door handle, tears well up in my eyes for the third time today. Damn, this must be a record for me. As I start trembling, George walks over to me and opens his arms. As he embraces me, I'm afraid I'll have the Harvey Bobson reaction again, but not this time. This time there is a warmth from the embrace, that outside of those from my parents, I've never felt before. I can feel that he really cares and wants to help me. After a few moments I break from the hug and thank him.

"I'll try to get over to the Center later this week," I say with a bit of hesitation in my voice.

"There's nothing to be afraid of, Josh. These people have gone through the same thing. They'll understand. But again it's your journey and your pace.

"Brad," I say with strength in my voice. "My name is Brad."

Smiling George replies, "Brad, there's nothing to be afraid of. I haven't known you long, but I can tell you're a bright young man with a strong personality and a good heart. There's more to you than you know. It's time you give yourself the chance to find the other part of you."

"I sure hope I'm ready," I say trying not to sound tentative.

"Have a good night, Brad. I'm glad you knocked on my door tonight."

"Me too"

As George drives off in his aging Ford Escort, I start the walk back to my dorm. As I'm walking, I hear humming and start to turn thinking there's someone walking near me. Suddenly I realize I'm the one humming and if I'm humming I'm probably more content than I've been in a long time. Holy crap. That's all it took to make me just a little bit happier. George is right; it's time for me to take control of my life and follow what my heart has been telling me. As I walk into my dorm room, I realize just what my heart is saying and I think I like it. I think I'm finally ready to listen.

6

"I do desire to learn, sir"

Entering my room I notice Jonathan's already asleep. This is something new. He's usually up chatting with his girlfriend at all hours of the night. Putting on my sleep pants, I disconnect my laptop and carry it over to my bed. I know it may not be the most accurate of websites, but I go to *wikipedia* and start looking for information on the Stonewall Riots.

I find myself mesmerized as I read about the revolt that started what is now known as the gay rights moment. I've gotta admit I had no idea how bad it really was for people back then. I think what amazes me even more is that in all the reading I had to do in school about the civil rights movement and Martin Luther King Jr., nobody ever mentioned persecution towards the LGBT community. I suppose that's typical, but it's still sad. One of the major parts of the Stonewall Riots

I don't know anything about is the transgendered community. I may know next to nothing about the gay community but I know even less about transgendered people. I guess at some point I'll work to figure that out too.

As I continue reading about the gay movement, one woman's name from the 70's keeps coming up, former Miss Oklahoma, singer and activist, Anita Bryant. She was a household fixture filling TV screens across America with orange juice commercials, but there was much more to her than that. She spent endless hours recruiting people to discriminate against gays. Stopping for a moment, I'm thankful that less of that goes on now, yet the next sentence I read reminds me that in many states in this country, you can still be fired for being gay. I mean actually *fired* for just being gay. That's pretty messed up. There doesn't have to be any other reason. It's just crazy, but as I'm learning everyday, life isn't fair and it seems even more so for gay people.

I have to keep reminding myself that so much has changed in a very little space of time. More states are allowing gay marriage and even the federal government is recognizing it. Even with those steps forward though I can't seem to bring myself around.

After hours of reading about the gay community and learning that lots of famous respected people like, Leonardo Da Vinci, who was actually arrested for sodomy, and Sir Francis Bacon, were probably gay, I decide it's time to hit the hay. But just as I'm about to close my eyes, I realize I'm nowhere near ready to go to sleep. I think back at the craziness of the day and remember I was supposed to have met Chris for lunch. Shit, I'm going to have to talk to him in the morning and apologize, but I better send him a quick text apologizing for not making it and check to see if he can do breakfast. Surprisingly, he responds quickly saying it's cool. I also really have to talk to Mary at some point as well. Damn, I've got a lot on my plate. Plus I've got to start writing the first draft for my film since I'll be shooting in less than a month and I haven't even come up with a storyline yet.

For the first time in long while I sleep through the entire night - no anxiety dreams. In fact, I don't remember dreaming at all. I wake up when the alarm goes off at 9:45 since I promised to meet Chris at the cafeteria at 10:30. In the shower I notice my shoulders starting to tense up and my stomach starts aching. I just don't think I'm ready to tell Chris but I'll wait and see.

As I head to the breakfast line, I take a quick breath as I notice Chris four people ahead of me. Like most typical college guys, me included, he has a tray loaded with food. Pancakes, eggs, bacon and actually some fruit; not bad for Chris. I get his attention and point to our usual table; he nods. So far so good.

"So, what the hell happened to you yesterday," Chris asks with a bunch of food still churning around in his mouth.

"Wow, not even the traditional good morning before, what the hell happened to you," I say with a smirk.

"Yeah, yeah, yeah. I know I'm class all the way but really, what happened to you, Brad? You've been totally out of it lately, man. Does this have something to do with Mary?" he asks.

"No, no, it's got nothing to do with her. I just kinda have a lot on my plate right now that I'm trying to juggle," I answer hoping to sound convincing.

"Why didn't you just say that's all it was yesterday when I saw you? You were acting like a douche, you know," he fires back.

What I really want to say is, "You know, Chris, what's really bothering me is that I've finally figured out I'm gay and it scares the shit outta me. I mean I know I should be cool and just roll with it, but I can't seem to shake the feeling it's wrong and that somehow I'll be less of a man when I tell everyone, especially you." Those aren't the words that come out though.

"Yeah, I know. Sorry, dude. I've just been wicked stressed with all the crap in my life right now. You know how it is," I apologize.

"Sure. Not trying to make a big deal outta it, Brad. I just want to you know that we're cool, that's all. Without turning this into some sort of bromace, you know I'm here for you, right?" Chris says.

I smile and say, "Aw, that's the sweetest thing you've ever said to me. I just might start crying right here," wiping imaginary tears from the corners of my eyes.

Chris picks up a piece of cantaloupe and throws it at my face. "But *you* would cry, idiot. You're the only guy I know who cries at the end of both *The Notebook* and *E.T.*

Feeling much better, I bring my hand to my heart and say, "Hey man, when E.T. says, 'I'll be right here' and touches Elliot's heart, that's deep; really deep," I counter with mock sentimentality and a smile.

"If you say so, dude. So come on, what's really stressing you out so much, Brad?"

I look down at my food trying to find the right words to tell him. Problem is I don't even know what the right thing to say is. After way too much silence I reply, "You know when there are those moments in your life when you think everything's piling up and there is no way you can handle all that's coming at you?" I ask.

"Yeah, I guess. I know you felt that way when you had your diabetic attack last year. Your parents didn't get into all the details, but I know that was a lot for you to deal with. Does this have something to do with your diabetes?"

"No, no, not at all. I'm just going through a rough patch right now and I'm trying to find out where I belong in the world," I say seriously.

"Where you belong in the world? What the hell's that supposed to mean?" Chris asks almost stupefied by my last statement

"I just don't know who I am right now and I'm trying to figure it all out while trying to stay friends with you, Laura and the gang, keep up my studies so I don't lose my scholarship, and figure out what I love most about film so I can get a frickin' job when I get outta of here."

"Well no offense, buddy, but with the exception of you trying to "find" yourself, we're all going through the same thing. But, hey, I get it. You don't have to tell me the specifics of what you're going through, but just know I'm here. We've been friends for a long time, but maybe you could talk to Laura. It might be easier with her."

I start to open my mouth to tell him but can't say the words. What if he does tell me it's okay, but it really isn't. I don't want to ruin anything with our friendship. Good lord, it seems like every time I take a step forward, it's then two steps back.

We sit talking for a while about school and other stuff when he brings up Mary.

"So, have you spoken with her since your date?" he asks.

Crap, I totally forgot to give her a call and apologize for everything. I need to do that right after breakfast. I give Chris some lame answer that I'm waiting a few days to build the excitement. He laughs and explains I better not wait too long or he'll move in himself and sweep her off her feet.

"Sorry, man, but I don't think you have a snowball's chance in hell with her," I say laughing at him.

"Well after being with you, she'll finally have the chance to be with a real man," he says laughing as he flexes a bicep.

"Pleez, dude, the only thing you tell girls is your shoe size and I know for a fact it doesn't coordinate with the size of your tackle."

"Hey, I have matured a lot since we went skinny dipping with the Neilson twins," he retorts.

I laugh remembering the summer after seventh grade when we went to a pond about a mile or so from my house. Chris had come over for a sleepover. It was really hot so we decided to head over for a swim early as the pond would get pretty crowded by midday. Jumping off our Huffy bikes, there they were, the Neilson twins. Debbie and Julie were already swimming. Now Chris really thought the twins were cute and by this time we were well out of the cooties faze and realizing that girls weren't all that bad.

It didn't take Chris long to throw off his shirt and jump into the warm July water. It took me a little longer. I'm not afraid of water, but I wasn't sure I wanted to be shirtless around the twins. Chris' torso and mine really weren't a match and I knew the girls would notice that.

After laughing and horsing around, the girls asked us whether we had ever gone skinny dipping. Chris gave a sly smile, winked and said we hadn't.

"Well, we've never seen boys' bits before. You want to show us," asked Julie coyly. Chris, always the negotiator, told them they had to take off their suits too. Never one to let up on his side of the bargain, Chris yanked his bathing suit off and ran into the water. I followed him in, leaving my suit on. The girls immediately dove under water to investigate. They came up giggling.

"Boy, everything looks bigger under water," said Debbie laughing.

"Okay, fair is fair," said Julie and the girls slipped off their suits.

Chris gave the biggest smile I had ever seen. He seemed more than pleased. I had always thought girls matured faster than boys, but the twins obviously still had a way to go. Chris, however, sure didn't seem to mind.

After a few minutes, the three of them got out of the water and headed into some nearby bushes to put their suits back on. Once dressed and sitting on the grass, Chris asked if I wanted to come out and have a soda and snacks with the girls. I explained I was going to stay in the water a little longer and would see them in a few.

"Suit, yourself," Chris said tossing back one of his great smiles as I treaded water.

Although the three of them had just played doctor, that was the extent of their sexual play. For the rest of the time they just ate and talked about what they were going to do with the rest of the summer.

I stayed in the water for another five minutes waiting for things to cool down. You see the second Chris took of his bathing suit, I started to get a boner. At first I thought it was the girls that were causing it but when he got out of the water and I saw both his front and back, I got ever more aroused. While waiting I tried to think of other things and it finally went down, but I was mortified.

After another hour or so at the pond we said good bye to the girls and Chris gave Julie a kiss on the cheek. As we were riding home, he couldn't stop talking about how much fun it was. I guess that was the first time I knew I was different from Chris and maybe from a lot of people.

I never talked about that time in the pond with anyone until Chris brought it up just now.

"Hey dude, *so* when are you going to talk to her?" he asks again.

"I haven't spoken to her yet, but I'll give her a call this afternoon," I say now back in reality of the moment.

"Why wait, Romeo? She's right over there."

And there she was, just two tables over sitting with a few of her friends eating and chatting away. I guess there's no really good to time talk to someone about a bad date. This might be as good a time as any to start growing some balls.

"Yeah, I probably should go talk to her. Thanks for listening, man. It means a lot," I say as I stand up and leave the table.

"Don't get all gushy, dude. It's cool. I gotta run anyway. Let me know how things go with Mary," Chris says as he picks up his tray.

Giving him a quick nod, I head over to Mary's table. She spots me and I see her leaning over to say something to her friends and who immediately get up from the table and head to an empty one a few rows over.

"Um, hey, how's it going? You mind if I sit?" I ask.

"Sure. Uh…yeah things are good. I have to go back for a few reshoots for Andy in a few days. Do you have to do anymore takes?" she asks.

"Naw. He hasn't said anything, but I'll help if he needs it."

"Listen, Brad. I don't want to go through tons of time not talking about the one thing I know is on your mind. First off, I have to apologize," she says with sadness in her eyes.

"Whoa, wait. Why are you the one apologizing? I'm the one who screwed the whole thing up," I say a little surprised.

"Well, I think I started rushing into the moment without thinking. Usually it's the guy that does that, but you were so nice to keep everything slow. I also shouldn't have made any assumptions of how you were going to react. You could have been ready in a little bit, but I pushed you. I also said something at the end I probably shouldn't have and I'm sorry," Mary continues.

The regret in her face is a little too much for me.

"Do you want to get out of here and go for a walk?" I ask.

"Sure," she says as she quickly chugs down her o.j. and grabs her tray and book bag.

We walk in silence for a little bit and then head over to the grassy area where I lost it just a few days ago. We sit under the same tree.

"First off, Mary, I want you to know I think you're a really great person and I'm really glad we had the chance to work on the film together."

"Yeah, it was great. I really thought it was going to be an awful experience, but you were such a gentleman," she replies with a sweet smile on her face.

Looking at her, I decide I need to tell her the real reason I went on the date with her in the first place. "Look, Mary, I did something pretty bad the other night and I need to tell you why I did it."

She looks at me with confusion but says, "I really doubt it was all that bad, Brad."

"You see, Mary, I went out on our date for a lot of reasons. One is that I think you are one of the sweetest, most attractive girls I've ever met and I did want to get to know you better. The other was I needed to find something out about myself and the only way to really do that was to go out on a date with someone like you."

"Brad, I have a feeling I know what you're trying to say and I'm guessing that you haven't really said it to all that many people. Sadly for you though, I'm not going to let you off the hook that easily. You need to say the words out loud."

I look at her and feel the tears start to well in my eyes. She moves closer and holds me for a second and we don't say anything to each other.

"I think...I think...I'm gay and I don't know what I'm going to do." After saying the words, my shoulders relax just a little. I hug her a little harder than I probably should. I can't believe I just said it. Maybe the fact that I don't know Mary all that well made it easier.

"It's okay, Brad. It really is. To be honest with you, I'm not thrilled that I was your "test subject" but I'm glad you chose to tell me. That's a brave thing to do, Brad. Maybe you are gay, maybe you're bi; it doesn't really matter. It's time though for you to find out who you are and learn to embrace it."

"But what am I going to do, Mary? I have to tell my friends, my family and then figure out what it even means to be gay. Shit, I wish there was a class that could teach me. Coming Out 101 or something. Hell, I always do well at school. I'd welcome the instruction."

Mary starts to laugh and hugs me again.

"Um, that's not the response I expected," I say a little surprised.

"Jesus, Brad, you're taking this all too seriously. Why don't you relax a little? You don't have to figure everything at once. Take a little time; tell people when you're ready. This is much more of a marathon than a sprint. You'll get there. Believe me I know a lot of gay guys. I'm a fruit fly," she says with a shrug and a smile." They all go through the same thing. You'll get there".

"Fruit fly?" I ask.

"Well it's a nicer phrase than 'fag hag'. It just means I'm good friends with a lot of gay guys. Actually speaking of that, I think you will do just fine in the gay community. You're good looking, smart, and a fresh face. You'll be great."

"We can still be friends, Mary, and you don't think I'm some kind of jerk for how I acted on our date."

"The important thing is you told me. That means a lot. Well, gotta run. I've got a class that starts in ten minutes, but remember," she says getting up from the grass. "I'm here for you."

"That's funny. You're the second person today to tell me that and speaking of that, I think my friend Chris has a big crush on you. Just thought you might want to know," I say giving her a little wink.

"Chris, huh? Well, he is pretty cute and his feet are huge. Maybe after you tell him, I'll give him a call. See you later, sweetie."

As she walks away I'm amazed at what just happened. God, this is the start I never thought would happen. I think this afternoon I'll head over and talk to George again. I sure have more to tell him than I thought I would at this point.

7

"Let me be that I am And seek not to alter me"

After a full day of classes, which included Modern European Governments, stats and a second level film production class, I'm exhausted but still need to meet George at his office.

Even though I want to meet with him, I'm still nervous as I walk through the doors of the Center. I know I don't have to worry, however, when looking up from his desk, he smiles as he gestures to the worn-out leather chair directly across from him. He seems pleased that I've made so much progress in such a short period of time. Telling Mary was a big part of that. I don't know where I'd be right now if she'd responded negatively.

"So, Brad, as much as I can advise with this, you really need to meet with someone your own age. There are a number of people here at the Center, but there's this one guy,

Kevin, I think you'd be really comfortable talking to. I hope its okay, but I did talk with him and he'd be willing to meet you when you're ready."

"Well, I don't even know anyone named Kevin so maybe that's a good thing," I say sort of hesitantly since I wasn't expecting this.

George hands me a sticky note with Kevin's contact information.

"I can't even stay much longer here, George. I've got so much to do for my film class, so I may not have a chance to text him till tomorrow at the earliest," I tell him.

"Not a problem, Brad. When you're ready, you're ready. He knows where you're coming from. That's the good thing. He's been there."

"Thanks again for everything, George. Please know this means a lot to me," I say as I get up to leave.

Walking down the stairs of the Center, I'm a little surprised with myself that I'm not bothered that George told someone else about me. Maybe it's another corner I'm turning.

Tomorrow comes pretty fast. It's Friday and thank god I only have only one class, astronomy. I do everything I can to stay focused and awake during the lecture about black holes or something, but my mind keeps wandering back to Kevin and what we're going to talk about. The 90 minutes drag on until class is finally over. Outside I check my blood sugar. Damn, I'm low so I head over to the convenience store on the south side of campus and pick up an apple juice and pack of *Nutter Butters*. The crackers stick in my throat as I wash them down with the juice. Already I know my blood sugars are getting back to normal, but my hands are still shaking from pure nerves as I pull out my phone to text Kevin. Digging into my jeans pocket, I pull out the crumpled paper with Kevin's number. I reassure myself. I can do this. I want to do this.

> *Hi this is Brad. George said I could give u a call. Can we meet some time?*

I hesitate for a few second and hit the send button. Per usual I start pacing, wondering if I did the right thing and if he's going to answer. I keep trying to reassure myself that he might be in the middle of a class or just not have his phone on. I know I shouldn't take a delayed response as anything negative, but I'm nowhere near as rational as I'd like to be. As these thoughts race through my head, my phone vibrates and my heart starts racing.

> *Hey Brad. Yup George mentioned u might call. Free rest of the day. Tell me when & I'll b there :-)*

Here I go again, Mr. Self Doubt. I have the chance to meet a gay guy who's my own age and make a connection, and I'm having second thoughts. Screw it! I'm going to do this. Go all in and take a chance.

> *THK. Can u meet in front of the observatory?*

In 15?

Sounds good. I'm wearing a blue/white striped polo.

Got it. See u in a bit.

I did it! Finally I did it. I picked the observatory because I know no one will be there now and it's pretty much the most secretive place on campus. I'm not sure I'm happy with my paranoia, but this is still so new to me and I have to go with what I'm feeling now. It doesn't take me more than five minutes to get to the observatory so I sit in front of the building and just people watch for a bit. It's towards the end of the day so there aren't too many kids wandering about. Still there are enough who are holding hands, being affectionate. Letting out a deep sigh, I know this is what I want. Something I've always wanted. I just need to believe it can happen with a guy.

I'm startled as I see a guy about my age standing in front of me blocking the sun. He's about six feet tall and has brown hair and blue eyes. I assume he's Kevin. He looks a little like Channing Tatum in *The Vow*. He's wearing tight black jeans and a plain grey tee shirt that shows that he obviously works out more than I do. It's still hard for me to admit, but I do really find him attractive and I suppose he's my type even though I'm not even sure what that is yet.

"Brad?" he asks looming over me.

"Yup, that's what my mom wrote on my underwear when I came here," I reply with a nervous laugh, as I stand up and extend my hand. He has a firm grip and I try to match it.

"Well at least you'll never have to worry about wearing your roommate's," he says with a broad smile. "Nice to meet you, Brad. You wanna head up to the top?" he asks gesturing to the front doors of the building.

Telling him that sounds fine, I secretly wish I had half the confidence he does. I pull my ID out of my wallet and slide it through the panel. Since I'm taking an astronomy class, I get access to the roof. Given the fact that the sun hasn't even set, there shouldn't be anyone on the roof. Hopefully, the perfect place when trying to be extremely private.

Walking through the lobby, I lead the way to the rooftop elevator. I push the button, the doors open immediately, and we enter and stand at opposite ends of the elevator. He looks at me and smiles but my return smile is apprehensive. What am I doing here?

Once we're on the roof I show him around a bit. It's pretty cool because it gives a tremendous view of the San Gabriel Mountains and you can also see the entire campus from here. On a clear day you can see all the way to downtown LA. This is a good day and there's not much smog. We look around for awhile. I point out my dorm and he does the same. There are benches around the perimeter of the rooftop and we sit down. We both know we didn't come here for the sightseeing opportunities though and after some small talk, he gets right down to it.

"So where are you in the process right now?" Kevin asks.

His voice seems calm and kind. He has no idea how much I appreciate that.

"Well, I'm not so sure what you mean. Didn't George tell you everything we talked about?"

Kevin looks at me curiously and smiles. Damn, wonder if he wore braces. He has perfect teeth.

"Actually George really didn't tell me that much. I figure your conversations with him are just that. Your conversations with me are the same. Let's just talk, Brad. You tell me everything you want and you can ask me anything too. I'm not here to push you and I'm sure no therapist. I think right about now you might need someone to talk to – maybe even a friend."

I lean back on the bench, smile at him and try to explain everything that's been going on for the last few years. It takes a bit of time, but he looks interested. He seems to be one of those active listeners they always talk about in pysch class. The kind of person who's paying attention to you all the time.

When I'm finished I relax a little, drained, but still needing to know about his experience. He explains that his wasn't all that different from mine. He had a few friends that didn't like the idea of him being gay so he told them he wasn't interested in staying friends with them. He came out in high school and kids were a lot rougher in his school than mine. He was shoved around some, but he said that happened with a lot of people, not just the gay ones.

"You know, Brad, bullying isn't just about us, but when I finally came out to everyone, most of them were pretty cool. I had some issues with my older brother, but like most brothers he came around."

"Okay, personal memoir time's over," he says with a smile. "What do you really want to know?"

"I'm...I'm not sure what you mean," I stammer.

"Come on, Brad. You haven't said it to anyone and probably haven't even said it to yourself, but deep down you're wondering what it really means to be a gay guy right?"

"I just don't know what I have to do. I mean how do I meet guys? Is it the same as meeting girls? What's it like walking into a gay bar for the first time? I mean, are there gender roles with gay guys? And, um, how do I know what position I'm supposed to be? Will it hurt?" I say letting go with a salvo of questions that have been bothering me for a long time.

"Okay, now you're getting to the things that are on most guys' minds. First off, Brad, you need to know there's no order in doing things. You can go out to a bar and still be coming out to people at the same time. Everything you're doing is just part of the process. Now let's start with gay bars. There are all sorts of bars out there for gay people and each one to some degree caters to a different clientele. You'll be nervous the first few times you go out because you'll be afraid you're going to get picked up right away or maybe no one's even going to look at you. One of the stereotypes of gay people is that we're always looking for the next guy. That's true and not true at the same time. If you keep your wits about you, you'll be fine and if you want I can go with you," he says.

"Wow, that'd be great, Kevin. Honestly, I'm not sure I'm ready to go it alone."

"Brad, you've asked a lot of the questions and they're really important ones, but I think there's something you haven't said to anyone and you need to get that out."

Looking up, I stare at this person sitting next to me. How can a person who has known me for literally less than an hour know the thing that's bothering me most in life? How can he know the thing that keeps me up at night and had me trying to kill myself? How can he know the thing that makes me want to cry all the time? How?

"I um…."

"Listen this is the hard part, Brad. I know that, but once you start saying it out loud you'll feel better, believe me. I know you don't want to say it, but you have to," he says softly.

I know I have to trust him. I take a few deep breaths and turn to him.

"I hate the thought of being gay. I hate everything about it. I've talked to George and my friend Mary and even someone at a hotline that helps people. I've even tried to convince myself that this is okay, but deep down I just can't be all right with it and I have no idea why. Kevin, I haven't even told my parents yet. I know they'll be okay with it, but there's always this doubt within me and I can't seem to shake it. This all seems like some kind of punishment. I don't understand what I've done to deserve this. One minute I feel like I'm moving forward and feeling better about myself and then the next I have such bad stomachaches that all I want to do is puke. I need to be fine with this because if I can't, Kevin, I honestly don't know what the fuck I'm going to do."

"There you go, Brad. Now that's what you were supposed to be saying from the beginning."

"What?" I ask, emotionally exhausted after my monologue.

"Yeah, Brad, this is the important stuff right now. It's not all about how to meet a guy at a bar. Not to say that's not something that's important. It is. But you'll have plenty of time to worry about that later. There's really just one thing you need to be worrying about right now and that's you. Forget about the rest of it. The first thing you need is to be comfortable with yourself. Now I want you to do something for me. It was something I had to do when I was coming out," he says moving on the bench to face me directly.

"Ah, okay. But, you're kinda making me nervous here. I'm not sure how ready I am for all of this," I say.

"Good! That's how you should be feeling. Now I want you to stand up and look me straight in the eye and say: My name is Brad…actually what's your last name?"

"Archer, Brad Archer. God, I've always wanted to say my name like 007," I respond with a smile.

Kevin gives a quick laugh and says, "Okay, I want you to say my name is Brad Archer and I'm gay. Can you do that and mean it? Remember if you can't, that's okay too."

"I don't know," I say looking down at my shaking hands. "I don't know if I can say it to someone I've only known for an hour. Give me a sec."

I walk to the other side of the roof. I close my eyes and try to open my mind to anything. The first thing that pops into my head is my parents holding hands and hugging. Then I see my high school friends and there I am in the cafeteria watching these kids flirting and exploring their adolescence and me doing nothing like that. Suddenly I realize how much I've given up remaining in the closet. I can go on blaming Harvey Bobson or those gay hating Christian Right groups or I can face the fact that although I'm strong in lots of ways, I haven't been strong enough to do the one thing I'm going to do now.

I walk up to Kevin, extend my hand and say out loud, "Hi, Kevin, my name's Brad Archer and I'm gay."

"Not bad, Brad. If this were an AA meeting, I think I'd have to give you a chip or something. Hey, that's what they do right?"

Then he does something I don't expect. He walks over to me and gives me a warm embrace. I find myself resisting.

"Don't fight it," he says warmly. "It's going to be okay, my friend, honest. There's nothing wrong with you."

"But…," I stammer.

"No buts, Brad. There's nothing wrong with you. There's nothing wrong with being gay and if people tell you different, those are their issues not yours. You're special. God made you gay and that's okay."

God made me this way. I've never heard someone say that before and it's nice to hear.

You're right, Kevin. It's time for me to be okay with it. I think it might be even time to tell one of my best friend's, Laura."

He leans forward and whips the tear from my cheek. I look down still a little embarrassed. He tells me it's all right to cry which reminds me of an album my mom and dad gave me when I was a little kid. It was called *Free to Be You and Me* and it had a song called "It's All Right to Cry". Sometimes it's amazing the things that pop into my head, but it all makes sense. Maybe crying does take the sad out of it, I think.

Kevin puts his arm on my shoulder as we get up from the bench and head to the elevator. On the ride down, he turns and smiles.

"Brad, you really are going to be okay."

"Thanks, Kevin. I mean it."

Leaving the building, I once again say thanks as we head to our separate dorms. Heading into my room, I realize how much has happened in the last 24 hours. It's a Friday night and my roommate's out. I don't have any plans, so I guess I'll just take a shower. As the water streams down my body, I start to think about Kevin. I close my eyes and imagine what it would be like to kiss him on the lips. During this fantasy I find myself getting hard. Without thinking, I start to stroke it slowly, imagining him holding me, lying on the grass, kissing passionately. It's only a few moments before I come. Although this is rather unexpected, I don't feel any shame in it. Wow.

8

"If you wrong us, shall we not revenge"

Wow! I'm kinda shocked at everything, but actually most of all from last night in the shower. I mean, obviously there have been a lot of telling signs that I'm gay, but actually feeling good when jerking off thinking about a guy in the shower, that's something new. Actually it felt *really* good and for the first time it felt right. No guilt. It's time for that guilt to stop. I also feel good about making a connection with Kevin and hope I can spend some more time with him.

After catching up on some shows I've missed lately like *Modern Family* and *Bob's Burger,* I decide to see if Laura's around to grab some lunch. After five rings she picks up.

"Hey, Laura, what's up?"

"Not too much. Just watching an old *Buffy* episode," she says

"Have you eaten yet?" I ask hoping she hasn't.

"Actually I haven't and was thinking of getting up off this bed and heading out to get something. You wanna join me?"

"Yeah. I've got a few things to do first so let's say 45 mins. I'll come by your dorm."

"Great! See you then," she says.

I hang up and for the next thirty minutes I keep trying to think of what I'm going to say to her and maybe more importantly, how I'm going to bring it up. I should have worn down the heels of my shoes with all my pacing and god, it's a wonder I have any skin left on my hands with all my hand wringing. I need to calm down. This is Laura I'm seeing. This is Laura I'm telling.

Pulling on a blue shirt and tan khakis, I head over to her dorm. It's an absolutely gorgeous day. I'm glad I left a little early so I can take my time and enjoy the nice weather. Southern California is one of those places where there really aren't a lot of seasons. It can be November and it's still 70 degrees out. Today's beautiful with just a little smog in an otherwise perfect sky. Now I just have to hope the rest of the day mirrors the weather.

After little debate we decide to go to *Palermo's*, a local restaurant which is known for their amazing pizza. It's in Los Feliz, not far from Hollywood. Not sure why, but I was a little afraid that the ride over was going to be awkward but lucky for me, Laura always has a great way of making me comfortable. She has this inner warmth that's very infectious. She's also extremely political and has no problem speaking her mind, especially if your opinion differs from hers, but we're usually on the same page with social issues.

Maybe I should give a little more background about Laura. First of all, she's around 5'5" and has a slim build. She has great legs, a killer smile and striking green eyes. She and I met early freshman year when we went to a sneak preview movie on campus. She happened to sit next to me and we reacted exactly the same way to the film. It was one of those comedies where everything is an awkward moment. We both hated it. Even though I didn't know her name, I felt an immediate connection to her and after the movie she asked if I wanted to get a hamburger at the pub on campus. I was more than willing to spend more time with her. Being around her was unlike anything I had ever experienced with a girl. It was later that semester that she asked me out and we went on a few dates. She introduced me to *Buffy the Vampire Slayer* and I introduced her to *007*. She had never seen a Bond film before and frankly I was stunned but allowed her the pop culture gap in her life.

Per the usual for me, the romance didn't last all that long but that wasn't for lack of trying on her part. At one point she told me maybe it would be better if we were just friends. I agreed and thought yeah, right, there was no way we would be able to just be friends after dating, but we have. Chris adores her as well and the three of us get along great and that's something that's really important to me.

Well, that's the back story of Laura and me and as we're waiting for the bread and soft drinks to arrive, our dating days seem far removed from the present. I've been able to make small talk for some time, but I know I have to get to the reason I asked Laura to meet me for lunch.

"Um, Laura, there's something I really need to tell you and I'm not sure how to do it," I say, totally unable to hide the nervousness from my voice.

"You aren't sick or anything like that are you," she asks with such worry on her face that I wish I hadn't seemed so nervous broaching the subject.

"No, no, it's nothing like that, Laura," I say trying to reassure her.

"Whew, that's a relief," she answers sweeping her hand across her brow with a mock gesture of relief. "I actually have something to share as well and now that I know you aren't sick, maybe I should go first."

"Sure," I say although I'm thinking that just when I get my courage up, she takes the lead.

Laura takes a big swig of water, leans across the table and takes my hand in hers and says, "I'm a lesbian, Brad."

In my peripheral vision I see the waiter heading to our table literally turn around and head the other direction.

After an audible gasp, I say, "Um, wow. A lesbian? I...uh. Wow. That's not what I expected to hear. I mean I don't get it; you're a hit with all the guys, Laura."

"Well, that's the thing really isn't it? I'm perfectly comfortable around guys and enjoy being with them, but when it comes to sex and making that *real* connection, I'm an absolute failure. But I've found that not to be the case with the ladies," she confesses with a slight shrug of her shoulders.

"God, I hope I wasn't the one that made you realize you're a lesbian," I say concerned. I mean I sure didn't make her feel sexually desirable.

"No, Brad," she answers with a slight smile. "I've actually had these feeling for a long time, but it wasn't till recently, when I met Rebecca, that I knew I was a full on dyke."

"You certainly have no problem using the terminology," I say smiling but still a little in shock. "Wait a minute...you just said Rebecca," I ask trying to process an actual partner for Laura.

"Sorry, sometimes I get so carried away in the excitement of telling people that I mention Rebecca without any lead in."

Seeing a lapse in the conversation the waiter returns and takes our order. Over a large pizza with mushrooms, Laura tells me about Rebecca and how they met.

"It was actually quite sweet. The cafeteria was really full and she had put her bag on the seat next to her without thinking. She saw me looking for a place to sit and signaled over to me. That was the start of it. We had a nice little chat over dinner and then decided we'd go to a poetry reading later that week. It was slow and romantic. We're still in the beginning phase of it all, but she's wonderful," she says warmly smiling.

Laura then gives me the story of how her parents were actually pretty amazing about it and so was the rest of her family. She considers herself very lucky. She seems so content with it all. However, I have to say that I'm still completely floored by the news.

"I've wanted to tell you for awhile, Brad, but for some reason I wanted to be sure things were going well enough with Becky before I said anything. I wanted to be sure I am who I am. I hope that makes sense," she says looking as serious as I've ever seen her.

"It does make sense, Laura, and believe me there are no judgments here," I say. "In fact I'm really happy you told me. It means a lot to me. It really does."

"I knew if there was going to be anyone of my friends I told first, it would be you, Brad. You see…"

Just as she is about to finish her sentence, I interrupt saying, "I'm gay, Laura."

She looks at me, puts her hand on my arm, smiles and says, "I know."

"Wait, what do you mean, you know?" I ask incredulously.

"Well, that's not quite the way I should have put it," she says wrinkling her forehead as she searches for the right words. "Over the past couple of months I've seen you acting differently and I know you've been working really hard to make a connection with a girl. You're also one of the most kind and loving people I've ever met, Brad. Take all of that combined with our dating experience and I had a slight feeling. Believe me it's not a bad thing when people say they know," she says reassuringly as she once again reaches across the table and touches my hand.

"I guess I want to believe that no one could ever imagine me being gay. I have this idea that if people know then I'm projecting some sort of stereotype of gay men and I don't want to be perceived through a stereotype."

"I get it, but you'll have to try and get past all of that at some point. I know you know this, Brad, but the people who love you will love you regardless of whether you're gay or not. The people that don't, they shouldn't be your friends in the first place."

She raises her glass of ice tea and says, "To being more than a stereotype."

We clink glasses and I smile. I'm feeling so much better about all of this. Chris had told me to talk with Laura and as usual he was right. Telling him though is going to be the tough part.

"Um, Laura, I kinda have of an issue though with telling Chris. I need to tell him everything and I think it'll be fine, but I also have some feelings for him that are more than just friendship ones. The problem is I know he's not gay, but I still have those feelings and I'm not sure how to handle them."

"Now we're getting into the tougher issues, Brad. You obviously need to tell him. The longer you wait, the better the chance he'll find out from someone else and you don't want that to happen."

"I know, I know. I just really want to stay friends with him, but I also have to try and get over the fact that I'm pretty attracted to him. I need him in my life, Laura. He's been there for almost as long as I can remember. I mean we both came clear across the country to Anderson partly because of our friendship."

"I don't want to tell you what you should or shouldn't do, but if it were me I would come out to him but save the attraction thing for another time. That can be a lot to take in all at once and does he need to know that now? If at some point you feel you need to tell him, then you should. Not everyone will take something like that well, so you never know, but you've been good friends for a really long time, so I have to imagine that in the end he'll understand and probably even be a little flattered. Actually knowing him, he'll probably love the fact that he's a hit with the ladies and the guys," she says with a laugh.

We talk for almost an hour and she tells me more about her coming out experience and what it's been like dating Becky.

"For the first time in my life I feel comfortable in my own skin and I love it," she says.

She seems to have really come a long way. It's a little sad to me though that she has stayed in the closet almost as long as me, but she certainly has progressed much more in the self-acceptance arena than I have. Driving back I ask her why she thought we dated in the first place.

"I think it was probably safe for both of us, Brad. We're both pretty easy to be with and very much non-threatening. For anyone who's struggling with his or her sexuality that can be a dream come true," she says.

"Hum, I guess that makes sense," I reply. "I'm glad I told you, Laura. Even though I've talked to a few people at the LGBT center on campus, it feels really good to know that one of my closest friends is there for me."

She tells me she feels the same and we agree that we'll always be there to support one another.

"I'm going to tell Chris soon," I say. "And what about you?" I ask. "He'll accept you, you know."

She assures me that she'll talk with Chris and after a nice long hug, I drive back to campus and park my car behind the dorm, head in and push the up button on the elevator. Waiting for the doors to open, I shake my head and smile. When life gives you lemons, make lemonade. Laura certainly helped me make a fresh batch this afternoon, I think, smiling to myself.

Feeling on cloud 9, I enter my room ready to get a little work done on the outline of my film. I think I finally have the germ of an idea. Walking in, I see that my side of the room is completely trashed. I've no idea what's happened until I turn to see my laptop and the paper taped to the screen with one large word written in red:

FAGGOT

I can't believe what I'm seeing. Stunned, I take the paper and place it on the desk. I want to rip it up, but decide I may need it later. Turning the computer out of sleep mode, I see the website I was looking at the other day. I hadn't been on the computer recently and realize it must have just gone to sleep mode leaving the webpage up. For whatever reason, my roommate must have gone on and seen it.

Trying my very best not to completely freak out, I start to put my clothes away. I grab a few tee shirts and notice that Jonathan has taken a black magic marker and written obscene words on most of them. I've never been close to Jonathan, but I never, ever expected he would do something as cruel as this. I put my clothes in a garbage bag, head back to my bed and pull back the blanket to find even more. Under the sheets I find my underwear, most of which has been torn to shreds. Others have words like "enter here" and "ass made for fucking" scrawled on the backside. He even took the time to cut slits in the back. Tears well in my in eyes as I clench my teeth. Grabbing everything he has destroyed, as well as my computer, I leave the room slamming the door behind me. Heading to the parking lot, I find my car and shove all the crap in the trunk. I know I'm going to need it if and when I go to administration.

I'm so pissed right now. Not only did Jonathan violate our space, destroy my room and attack me for being gay, he also ruined one of the happiest days I've had in a long time. My hands shaking, I text Kevin telling him I really need to see him and can he meet me soon. It takes about five minutes for Kevin to text me back, the longest five minutes ever, but he replies "Yes. How about I pick a place?" Tired of texting I dial his number.

"Hello," he answers.

"Hey there. I thought it would be easier to call. If we could just have a little time to chat before we get there, that'd be great," I say trying not to sound as angry as I am.

"Yeah, yeah sure. No biggie. I gotta change but I'll meet you in the parking lot by your dorm in twenty minutes."

"Sounds good. I need to do something quick before we leave," I respond.

First off, let me explain that I'm not the type of person who normally believes an eye for an eye. I know I could do awful things to his stuff just like he did to mine and believe me there is a part of me that wants to open his closet and piss all over his things. But, I can't do that. Neither can I just let this go. It seems to be a pretty quiet late afternoon and no one's in the hall. Finding Jonathan's still out, I calmly walk around the room and open his drawers until I find his underwear. The funny thing is he has all types of underwear including bikini briefs. I take all of them – even the ones in his hamper. Grabbing a few sheets of paper, a marker and duct tape (Thanks, Dad) I move out to the hallway. Quickly I tape every pair to the wall and at both ends of the display, I list Jonathan's full name and his cell phone number followed by:

ALL MY UNDERWEAR IS FREE. SORRY FOR
THE STAINS! ENJOY!!

Finished I head back into the room and take everything I can that I think he might destroy. Done, I head back to my car, leave my things in the trunk and wait for Kevin to arrive.

Pulling up he can't miss the grin on my face.

"You seem pretty happy. What's up?" he asks.

"Not much. I just had to get rid of some clothes and it felt really good."

9

"Oft expectation fails, and most oft where most it promises"

During the ride to West Hollywood, I try to explain everything to Kevin. Talking it out, I realize this has to be one of the weirdest days ever, with one of my best experiences so far in telling Laura and then ending with my prick of a roommate destroying my stuff. As bad as that was, the homophobic slurs everywhere hurt much more. It's pure hatred with little reason behind it. Looking at Kevin, I can see he's almost as angry as I am.

"So what did you do when you saw all your stuff like that?" Kevin asks with obvious concern.

"For starters, I took his all underwear and taped them to the corridor wall outside our room with a sign announcing that anyone who wanted them could take them – stains and all."

Kevin laughs for a second and then his expression changes quickly. "You do know that there are going to be repercussions for what you did, Brad, and they're not just going to be coming from your roommate. The administration might find out and you'll have to deal with that too," he says seriously.

"Wow, Debbie Downer. You know what, Kevin, I don't want to think about it. Right now, I'm here with a great guy, heading out to my first gay bar. I want to focus on that instead of my dumb ass homophobic roommate."

"Fine by me," he says with a smile. "Maybe you're right. Tonight should be about forgetting the bad and having some fun. Just know that it'll be all there waiting for you when you get back."

After a few moments of silence, I suddenly get nervous. Sure I'm, talking big but am I really ready to go to a bar and possibly be hit on by guys? Even though I know I really shouldn't be drinking with my diabetes, I'm going to need something to get through tonight.

"So...um what kind of bar are you taking me to," I ask basically completely unaware of the whole gay bar scene.

"I was actually thinking about that while I've been driving. I wasn't quite sure where to take you. No offense, Brad, but I figure you're probably pretty clueless about the gay bar scene. There are all kinds of bars catering to different people. I was going to take you to a leather bar where there are a bunch of hairy older men, but I decided to pass on that this time around," he says with a smile.

"Come on, Kevin; cut me a little slack here."

"I keep forgetting we don't know each other all that well. I tend to be pretty sarcastic so you shouldn't take me all that seriously."

As we sit at a red light on the corner of Crescent Heights and Santa Monica Blvd, he pauses for a moment and then turns to me.

"I thought we'd go to a bar that caters to people our own age, one that's not too loud. I figure we'll want to chat. As the night goes on, things will get a little bit crazier, but you'll be fine. By the way, why did you want to go to a bar tonight of all nights?"

"I really don't know," I answer with a shrug of my shoulders. "When I was getting back at Jonathan, it was just a complete visceral reaction. I wasn't even thinking. I just did it. I'm probably doing the same thing here. Right now I'm just going with the flow, seeing where the world takes me. Not sure drinking is the most effective way to accomplish what I need right now, but at least I'm going out and doing something I haven't done before. It's all about trying new things, right?"

"Just know that people like your roommate are few and far between. Most people are pretty tolerant towards us. I also believe in karma. He'll find out the error of his ways someday," Kevin answers as he studies me seriously. "You know the old saying: 'what goes around, comes around'."

"Yeah, I guess so. I'm not very good at all though with confrontational situations. I'm hoping things on the horizon will be better," I answer with a sigh.

Suddenly Kevin quickly does a u-turn in the middle of the street and parallel parks in a tight spot. Needless to say,

I'm not a frequent visitor to West Hollywood but it seems to me that we aren't all that close to the bars. There are lots of closed shops around but nothing that would seem like the gay bar scene.

"It will better, Brad. Believe me. Well, we're here so you can stop ringing your hands now. Don't worry. You'll be fine. You're with me."

Before I open the door, I have some thoughts about him protecting me and I have to admit they're pretty erotic. I don't know him all that well, but he seems to be the kind of guy that I'd want in my corner and it feels good. Maybe a little too good.

"Come on, dude. Let's do this thing," he says with a sly wink.

"Um, yeah, just give me a second. I need to test my blood sugar."

I take out my tester and check my blood, which is good at 127, but I'm also rearranging my crotch since I got a little aroused thinking about Kevin. Thank god I'm wearing jeans. A few seconds later and I'm good to go. Getting out of the car, Kevin looks over at me with a knowing smirk. Knowing I've been caught, my face turns beet red, but he puts his hand on my shoulder immediately relaxing me.

It's a nice night. There's a full moon and you can actually see a few stars in the sky. It's pretty warm, around 68 degrees - a perfect LA night.

"As you can see, there isn't much parking near the bars so we'll have to walk a little way to get there. For some reason this is the way it's always been in West Hollywood," Kevin explains.

"So how do you think I look?" I ask. "Do I look ready for my big splash?" I'm dressed in black jeans and a button down long sleeve black shirt.

Laughing, Kevin says, "Well, you know what they say, Brad, black is slimming."

"Hey," I retort giving him a slight push.

"Just kidding. You look great. As a newbie you are going to do just fine tonight. Don't worry about it. I'll take care of you, Brad. Just relax and have some fun."

Last year a friend got me a fake ID that's always gotten me into bars with friends. I don't really drink all that much and when I do it's mostly on campus. Part of the reason I don't do a lot of the bar scene is that I'm not all that confident around women in those situations. I'm always afraid I might get hit on. Thinking about that now though is quite an ego boost. It'll be interesting to see if I feel the same way around guys.

After about five minutes of walking, we reach the bar called GUYS (an appropriate name).

"So this is it, Brad. I figured we'd go here and see where the night takes us. Obviously this place is pretty much just for guys, as the name implies. There are a few lesbian bars around as well, but not as many as you'd think. I know it seems a little quiet right now, but the place will start to hop in a bit. There's usually some loud music later on and they open up the roof so people can dance outside," he tells me as he guides me through the doors and into the bar.

We find a spot in the middle of the room and take a seat. I start looking around with some apprehension. The walls are adorned with televisions that show some of the upcoming events at the bar but also with scenes from some very graphic porno videos.

"So is having streaming porno commonplace at bars around here," I ask trying not to look too obvious as my eyes dart around the room

"Probably not at straight bars, but here it's pretty much standard. If it bothers you, you can always have my seat looking away," Kevin says before asking me what I want to drink.

"I have no idea," I answer still overwhelmed by the surroundings. "When I do drink, I'm sort of a Stella man, but I guess I'll have whatever you're having."

"Hey, Marty," Kevin yells out to a cute waiter walking by.

He heads in our direction and like most of the wait staff here he's shirtless and wearing tight pants. He's extremely good looking with abs that would make Taylor Lautner jealous.

"Hey, Kev, what's up?" Marty says sharing a fist pump with Kevin.

"Not much. Hey, Marty, this is my good friend, Brad. He's new to the scene. Tonight's his inaugural night out on the town and I want to make him comfortable."

"Haven't seen such fresh meat in a long time," says Marty looking me over. "You're a good looking guy, Brad. But listen, try not to get caught up in all of this. And now for the really serious business," he says with a wink. "What'll you have?"

"Go on, Kevin," I say deferring to him.

"We'll have two madrases, Marty."

"Sounds good. Be right back with those."

"So what's a madras?" I ask him as my eyes follow Marty and his tight pants as he walks to the bar.

"It's actually a pretty simple drink. It's vodka, orange juice, and cranberry juice. Basically a screw driver with cranberry."

A few moments later Marty comes back with the drinks and Kevin lifts his glass.

"To my good friend Brad. I hope your first time out is nothing short of amazing. Welcome to the club," Kevin says.

I'm thinking Kevin and Marty must be pretty good friends as the drinks are pretty strong. I give myself a little insulin as I'm pretty much drinking sugar.

"Yeah, Marty and I have been friends for a little over a year. This was the first bar I went to in West Hollywood and I was probably more nervous then you are right now. I sat down at the bar with my head down. Marty was so sweet. He offered me a drink on the house and since it was a Tuesday night and not all that busy, he just started chatting. He introduced me to a lot of his friends and after his shift showed me the good and bad bars in town. Of course, he thinks his bar is the best," he says. "When I first came out and started becoming confident with myself, I tended to get a little carried away. I was lucky that there weren't any long lasting consequences."

"I'm not sure what you're getting at," I ask.

"Well, I don't want to give you a bad impression of the community, but there are some real issues. Drugs and unprotected sex happen all too often. A lot of guys get into meth. It's an easy escape, Brad, and it also keeps you thin, another big deal in the gay community."

"Not interested in drugs, Kevin, so there's no real issue there – well with the exception of a little pot now and then," I say with a knowing smile.

"Never say never, my friend. Just stay smart. Lots of people tend to rush into things when they first come out. They get lost in the lifestyle and some don't always have the best coming out experience and end up using drugs as an escape," Kevin explains with a tone more serious than anything I've heard him say yet.

For whatever reason, this starts to bother me and Kevin can see it.

"Okay enough serious talk. Let's play a little game and rank all the people coming into the bar. One is as ugly as can be and 10 is an Adonis," Kevin explains.

This is actually kinda fun as I've never really thought of men this way. I suppose it's pretty superficial, but what the hell. You're allowed that every once in awhile. Suddenly a tall and rather sexy latino guy comes into the bar. He's gotta be around 6 foot and looks like he must be a hit with the guys.

"Now that man is a definite 9.5 and I mean that in every way possible," Kevin says smiling at me.

As the night moves on, I'm starting to get a little buzzed and am certainly starting to feel the vodka. Kevin tries his best to slow me down, but I'm having none of it. I want to party. Just as I'm starting to get pretty drunk, two of Kevin's friends arrive. Instant buzz kill.

"Brad, I want to introduce two really good friends, Tyler and Blake," Kevin says smiling glancing at his two buddies.

I timidly rise from my seat to shake their hands. Blake and Tyler look like average college guys. They're both pretty cute. Blake's around 5'10" with green eyes blond hair and a swimmer's build. Tyler is black and a little taller with brown eyes and what seems to be a bit stronger build. They obviously seem like okay guys, but they're taking away my time with Kevin. I'd like to think I'm not too selfish a guy but I really wanted and needed alone time with him, not only to get to know him, but to have the support I really need tonight. I mean this was a really shitty afternoon and the alcohol is making me a little morose.

As the night goes on, the drinks keep flowing. Having been at the bar for a couple of hours now, I'm really drunk and opening up more than I probably should. Tyler and Blake ask the two of us if we're interested in another round. Kevin says we're good, but water would be nice. Again buzz kill, I think, acting like I'm interested in anything that Tyler and Blake are saying.

At this point I've attained a generous amount of liquid courage and with Tyler and Blake away ordering at the bar, I decide to do something either outrageously brave or crazy.

"You know you look really hot tonight, Kevin," I say with as much sexiness in my voice as I can muster.

"Aw, thanks, Brad, but I think the alcohol's doing a lot of the talking right now," he says with much more clarity than I have right now.

"No, no. I mean it, Kevin. I haven't really had all that much time to think about who's hot and who's not, but tonight I know you're wicked hot," I continue on a definite roll now.

"Well, er, that's…um…nice to hear, Brad, but…"

Before he has the chance to say anything else, I take the initiative and lean over and kiss him full on the lips but before the kiss can go anywhere, Kevin pulls away.

"Whoa, slow down there, cowboy," he says with a look of complete shock.

"Um, well…I…thought that you and I were hitting it off and well…" I say fumbling over my words like a complete idiot.

"Brad, you're a great guy and you're really cute, but I just don't have those same feelings for you and we really just met. You have to take your time and figure out a few things before you start with this."

"I…I just thought you might be the one," I tell him my face turning red.

"Brad, I think that's the alcohol talking. Hey, why don't I get you some water and we'll talk some more. Okay? I don't want to hurt you, Brad. I really want to help and be your friend. That's what you need right now. Honest," Kevin says as he pushes his chair away from the table.

"I get it," I say with an audible sigh. "Maybe some water would be a good idea."

Kevin gets up and puts a reassuring hand on my back which I push away. I don't want to be touched by him right now. Once he gets lost in the crowd, I make sure I have all my stuff, leave a twenty on the table, and head for the exit. At the door I turn around and see him looking for me. For a split second I contemplate heading back but decide against it. I don't need anymore of this right now.

Walking down the street, I immediately realize that I'm completely wasted. I can't seem to walk straight and I have no idea where I'm heading and since Kevin drove over here, I have no way of getting back. Damn, I need to find an ATM so I can get some cash and a taxi.

Suddenly I get an unbearable urge to pee and there's no real place to go. There's another gay bar just up the street that has a line forming outside but there's no way I can wait that long so I make a beeline for a dark alley. Am I really doing this? This is so unlike me, but then again who the hell am I anyway?

While I'm taking care of my business, I notice someone coming down the alley. I quickly turn my body, facing the opposite direction of whoever it is.

"Hey, buddy, it's no big deal. I'm not a cop. I'm just here to do the same thing. Some time the lines in bars are fucking ridiculous and after five beers I can't wait that long."

My speech slurred, I try to tell him I feel the same way. Zipping up, I turn and look at him. He's about my age and great looking. He probably even goes to Anderson.

"You know I was rejected by someone tonight. I feel like I put my heart on the line and he just ignored it," I tell him throwing my arms in the air.

"That sucks! Believe me I've been there. Say, my name's Bobby."

He wipes his right hand on his pants and I do the same and we shake hands.

"Well, I'm not all that interested in heading back to the bar. I'm gonna take Uber back to campus. You interested in sharing one?" he asks.

"Uh, yeah, that'd be cool, but I don't have any cash for you. You think we could hit an ATM?" I ask.

"Don't sweat it, bud. I'm sure we can figure out a way you can pay me back," he says reaching down and grabbing my crotch.

I'm so gone I don't even care. Putting my arm around his shoulder to help support myself, we walk out of the alley. After a few minutes on the curb he raises his left arm to let the Uber car know it's for us. Stumbling into the back seat, I'm beginning wonder if this is the right thing to be doing? God damn this has been a shitty day and I'm so drunk right now.

10

"What's done cannot be undone"

The ride back to campus is pretty much a blur. I'm sure Bobby was talking about all kinds of stuff, but I have no idea. All I remember is his kissing me as we get out of the car. His breath smells like stale beer. Ugh.

My balance is way off and I almost fall getting out of the car. Bobby guides me along the sidewalk, putting my arm around his shoulder and holding my side with his other hand. For some reason I have the inclination to talk to everybody that walks past us telling them to have fun, but be safe. I even yell "Hey, hottie!" to one girl walking by.

"Maybe it's better if we go back my place," Bobby offers.

"Sounds like a plan," I mumble. "All this walking is making me really dizzy, really tired and really, really horny," I say with a foolish grin on my face as we walk to the front of some building I'm too drunk to recognize. Bobby rests me against the side of the building as he fishes out his key card.

Inside Bobby pushes the button to the elevator and smiles as he kisses me on the cheek. God, I really have no idea which building we're in. Guess I haven't been paying all that much attention. I'm sure when I sober up a little bit, I'll find my way back to my room. Boy my roommate's gonna be pissed when I get back. Oh well.

"So are you too drunk to have some fun," Bobby asks with a hint of seduction in his voice.

"No, no, no, not at all," I reply. "You want to play a board game or sumthin?"

Laughing, he leans over closer to me, "Um that wasn't exactly the type of fun I was thinking about. How about you relax and I'll take care of you."

Suddenly he reaches down and starts to unbutton my pants.

"You know before we go any further I think I outta tell you something," I stammer.

Before I can finish he's pulled out my dick and starts giving me a blow job. I'm really, really drunk, but this is fantastic. I mean I've never felt anything like this before. No wonder everyone makes such a big deal out of it. The ecstasy of the moment combined with the liquor almost makes it feel like an out of body experience I never want to end. I keep moving my head around in circles moaning.

After what seems like eternity, but must have been only a few minutes, Bobby stops, gets off his knees and slides next to me on the couch.

"Well, I got you off to a good start. Now I think a little reciprocation is in order," he says smiling as he pushes me towards the floor and onto my knees while he begins unbuttoning his pants. I'm not sure what he means until I see him pull down his pants.

For whatever reason, I instinctively know what to do. I slowly start to rub his dick which is pretty big. He slowly begins to moan and tells me to suck. I slowly go down.

"Hey there, little buddy, watch the teeth," he says as I look up at him.

"Sorry," I mumble. Once in a rhythm I can see he's starting to really enjoy it. God, I hope I remember I'm good at this, I think.

Suddenly he pushes my head off him, lifts me up, and turns me on my back on the couch. He pulls my legs in the air taking my pants, shoes and socks off and then tears my shirt.

"Be right back, lover boy," he says with a little laugh.

Suddenly he just up and leaves only to return a minute later grabbing me by the waist and bending me over the side of the couch. Still very much out of it, I start feeling something cold around my butt and I'm not sure what's going on.

"Whoa, whoa…wait a second," I tell him momentarily more alert than I've been all night.

"Don't worry. You're really drunk. You probably won't even feel a thing," he says. "Just take a sniff of this and relax."

He puts something right underneath my nose and in my stupid, drunken state, I inhale deeply. I'm suddenly very light headed and aroused.

"What the hell did you just give me?" I ask bewildered.

"Are you serious? You've never had poppers before?" he asks with genuine disbelief.

"I thought I told you. I've never been with a guy before. I swore I told you all of this in the cab," I say starting to get angry.

"Yeah, right," he says sarcastically. "Oh I love when cute boys like you pretend it's their first time. It makes it all the more exciting for me."

"No, honest. You see you're the first guy I've ever done anything with and I just don't think I'm ready for whatever you're about to do," I reply anxiously.

"Oh believe me, you're ready for this," he says grabbing my hard dick.

With little foreplay he inserts a finger and I inhale deeply, surprised and a little scared. Thinking I'm ready, he rather quickly and unceremoniously inserts his dick. Even though I think I felt him using some kind of lube, the pain is still excruciating.

'Ah! Bobby! You've got to stop! I can't take," I scream while bucking to get him off me.

"Stop squealing, you little bitch. I'm only halfway in. And please, don't pretend you aren't enjoying this. Just breathe slowly, push out a little and you'll be fine. God, you are tight," he says.

Suddenly I'm very much out of my drunken state. Bobby now has established a rhythm and I scream again.

"Dammit! You need to take it out or slow down. I can't take the pain. You're tearing me apart!"

I continue to squirm trying to get him out of me. With a frustrated sigh he does slow down and for the first time, it starts to actually feel good.

"Jesus, there you go. I knew you'd finally get into it," he says looking a lot less frustrated than before. His face is one of someone with complete control. It's almost animal-like, teeth gritted.

Finally he climaxes and so do I. I'm relived for three reasons. First, that it's over with, second, it was pretty good towards the end and third, I just saw Bobby throwing out a condom. That whole thing hadn't even occurred to me until he started to walk away.

Lying there I wonder what I just did. I couldn't have done this. This is not what my first time was supposed to be like. I wasn't supposed to have been picked up by a stranger and gone to his place. It was supposed to be romantic. Did I really want this? This is so out of character for me - Mr. Good Guy, Mr. Follow the Rules. Everything happened so quickly. Where the hell am I anyway?

From another room, I hear the toilet flush and Bobby, right his name is Bobby, saunters back like he just won a basketball game. Arrogant.

"Well, I have to tell you, Brad, that was pretty fucking amazing."

"Yeah, I guess it was good. Do you think we could just talk for a few minutes? I need to wrap my head around all of this." I say feeling like I need to make some sort of connection with him on an emotional level.

"What's there to talk about, dude? We just had some amazing sex and now you're going to head back to your dorm so I can get some sleep and sober up. Maybe I'll call you some time."

"Whoa, whoa, wait. What?"

"Come on, man. I picked you up off the street. You can't imagine this was going to be anything but a good fuck. Right?"

"I'm not sure what I thought it was going to be but I certainly didn't expect to be thrown out of your place after giving you my virginity," I say feeling my throat tighten and the anger starting to well up in my face.

"Yeah, right. Take away your virginity. You know what, buddy, that line might work well in the moment but after we're finished it's gets a little old."

I get up slowly. I'm tired, sore and already starting to feel hung-over. I look around the room and see a small fridge in the corner. I open the door, look inside and remove a bottle of Corona and toss it on his lap.

"You know what, Bobby? I was extremely drunk and probably still am a little, but when someone tells you it's their first time, you might want to consider the fact that it actually might be the first time. And when they tell you to slow down because it hurts like hell, you may want to take that into consideration too. You wouldn't want someone reporting you for raping them just because they asked you to slow down or stop and you didn't. And I certainly didn't want my first time to be with some dipshit I met in an alley. And by the way, why don't you take that Corona and shove the whole thing up your ass, because that's what it felt like," I say turning to leave.

He looks at me and stammers, "Wait, what are you gonna do?"

I take a moment before I turn to face him. "Well I was pretty stupid in all of this. Why don't you try and be less of an ass and listen to the person you make love to? It certainly will get you in less trouble. And by the way, if I gave you my number, you can delete it. I don't think I'll be picking up if you call."

Walking out of his room, I feel like all I've been doing for the past six hours is get angry. The real issue probably isn't even with everyone else but with me. I'm the one that needs to get his shit together and step up and be the person I should be. But right now I need to figure out what dorm I'm in and how to get back there.

Once outside I realize that my dorm is only a few minutes away. There's a breeze in the air which helps clear my head and give me some clarity. Clarity's not something I've had all that much of lately. Right now though I need to crawl into bed and deal with everything in the morning – which is probably only a few hours away. As I walk, I think of the line from Shakespeare 'Oh what fools we mortals be.' Couldn't have said it better myself, Will. Couldn't have said it better.

With the elevators shut down for repair, I have to climb the three flights to my floor which seems to take a hell of a lot longer than usual. Fumbling around in my pants pocket, I finally find my keycard. I open the door and a fist comes flying towards my face. I stumble backwards as my head slams against the wall and then there's complete blackness.

11

"Boldness be my friend"

I'm walking through the woods heading towards a lake. The lake is the one I went to many times with my parents and extended family. It's so familiar to me, which is pretty strange since I haven't been here in maybe five or six years. Leaving the clearing, there's a small beach ahead of me with a section leading upwards and what seems to be a large boulder off to the left. I remember sitting on that rock when I was a kid and having moving conversations with my grandfather. He was an amazing man. I sure wish I could talk to him right now. Somehow I think he'd understand.

It's a beautiful summer day and I take off my shoes and socks and dip my feet into the warm water. I have shorts on so I'm able to wade in up to my knees. Suddenly I feel like I'm being watched by someone. Turning around, I see an older man sitting on the boulder. He looks like my grandfather, but he can't be him. Papa died four years ago.

Despite that, I walk slowly up the wooden plank walkway to the rock I so loved as a child. As I get closer, I squint and do a double take. It really is my grandfather, but not my grandfather when he died, but him about fifteen years earlier.

"Papa?" I ask with both confusion and happiness in my voice.

"Hi, Brad. It's so good to see you, son," he says, smiling and tapping his hand on the rock as he beckons me to sit beside him. A little nervous, I comply and sit with just a small distance between us.

"But…you're….I mean you're…" I say, my voice shaking.

"Dead? Of course I am. But that doesn't mean I can't come and see you when I know you need me," he says with a smile I so loved.

"Um…does this mean I'm dead too?" I ask hoping against hope that my question is wrong.

"No, you aren't dead, Brad. You have a long way to go before you reach your time. Nope, I'm here to talk about what you're dealing with right now."

More comfortable, I slide over closer to him. Lord knows how long I'm going to have with him. I want to make the most of it; whatever it is.

"You see, Brad, I've been watching you. I've always kept an eye on you because you've always been so important to me. We had a bond I don't think a lot of young men have with their grandparents and I've always been so proud of everything you accomplished…until now," he says with a hint of concern.

"Oh, god. You mean you saw all the stuff I just did," I answer, my face reflecting my sadness.

"Don't worry. I only see the stuff I really need to and it's all pretty much PG," he says with a wink of his still crystal blue eyes. "But that doesn't matter. You seem to be spiraling a little here, Brad, and I'm here to explain a few things and let you know something you've been wondering about but haven't said to anyone. Actually, you haven't even said it to yourself," he replies looking straight at me.

"Papa, I'm doing the best I can. I mean I really am. This is so hard. There's so much more to all of it. Sometimes I feel great and sometimes I feel really, really awful. Part of me wishes I was still the little boy sitting on this rock with you summer after summer."

He looks at me and smiles. His smile is something I'll always remember. Whenever he cracked that grin, I couldn't help but do the same.

"I'm here to tell you the thing you need to hear, Brad. It's okay. It's okay to be gay. It's who you are, but now you have to accept it and be happy."

"Deep down I know that, Papa. It's just convincing myself that's making this so hard," I answer, my words catching in my throat.

"It's time for you to tell Chris, your friends, and your parents, son. They'll be supportive and still care for you. But that's not all, Brad. There's one more thing I need to tell you that you've been wondering about since that time you were in the hospital a few years ago," he says with thoughtfulness in his eyes.

As we talk, a shaft of light emerges from behind a cloud and illuminates the lake in front of us.

"Well, I know you love me and trust me, but I figured I needed to show you a little something beforehand. It's not just me speaking to you, Brad. I have God with me as well."

"You have God with you, Papa? What do you mean?"

"Well, let's just say He's a busy man and today He's allowing me to speak on His behalf. He just wants you to know that He's okay with it too," Papa says with a comforting voice.

"Papa, this is an awful lot to take in and I just don't know if I believe in all of this. I mean I have a hard time thinking God is here right now."

"Well, I understand that, Brad, but remember this. Did I ever lie to you?"

"No, Papa. I trusted you more than almost anyone. You'd never lie to me."

"Well, then, Brad, trust me now and just listen. You know there's a lot of mumbo jumbo in the Bible, but in the end all God wants from you to be is true to yourself and be the good, kind, caring young man we both know you are. Don't worry about what God thinks about you being gay. He's okay with it and now it's time for you to be. I love you, Bradley, and I miss you. So does Nanny. Chris is waiting for you now. Why don't you tell your best friend," he says, his voice starting to fade.

"I will and I love you, Papa. I miss you. I wish you could stay," I say as tears fill my eyes. And then he's gone, just slipped away.

Suddenly I hear my name being called as if in the distance.

"Brad, Brad."

"Papa," I say.

I'm awake. Everything's blurry and it takes a few moments for me to get my bearings. As my eyes focus, I realize I'm in a bed in what appears to be a hospital, but what the hell am I doing in a hospital. How did I get here? Why am I here? As I turn my head to the side, I'm greeted with a wave of nausea from the throbbing pain in my head. To my left is Chris, smiling down at me.

"Since you've been sleeping for awhile, I figured I'd give you a little shake to see if I could wake you. Don't worry. I didn't hit the side with the shiner on it," Chris says with a playful smirk.

"Huh, what the hell happened? Why the hell am I here, Chris?" I ask totally confused.

"Well, my dear friend, you had your face punched in by your adorable roommate. You hit the back of your head against the wall and were knocked out. He must have hit you pretty hard for that to happen. Apparently the little shit got nervous and ran. Someone heard the commotion and called security who took you to the on-campus medical center and they brought you here. I must be your emergency contact because they called me and here we are," Chris explains.

"I appreciate it, Chris, but the real question is why does my head hurt so much? Aren't they supposed to pump me full of drugs so I don't feel anything?" I say with a small smile that makes my face hurt even more.

"Boy, you are a drama queen," Chris says with a small laugh. "Not sure how many nurses are here in the wee morning hours, but I'll go let them know that you're awake."

Once Chris is out of the room, I take few moments to think about the dream I just had. Was it all really just a dream or was my grandfather/God telling me something? But that'll have to go on the back burner because right now I have to tell Chris about what happened tonight. Do I make up some cock and bull story or do I just tell it straight? Pun intended.

"Hey, buddy, look who I brought back," Chris says as he walks in with a very cute male nurse. "Sadly all the cute girls worked the last shift," Chris says smiling.

"Hi, Brad, my name is Dylan and I'm actually the nurse on duty," he says giving a smile to Chris. "The doctor has agreed to give you some Tylenol that will help with the pain. We can't give you anything else due to the concussion and some bleeding in the back of your head. Now I need you to follow this light.

I look up, down, left and right and am even able to name the President and First Lady.

"Um, Dylan, why do I need to have a drip?" I ask.

"Well, when you came in you were pretty dehydrated and this way we can hydrate you quickly. Now take these pills, one of them will help with your nausea and the other is just Tylenol" he explains as he checks the bag hanging beside the bed.

As Dylan leaves the room, I look at Chris and smile.

"I really gotta tell ya something, Chris," I say fighting the overall tiredness I'm feeling.

"Are you sure you wanna do that, Brad? It's been a long day and I'm guessing you're pretty tired. Why not just rest," he says with concern.

"Believe me, Chris. I'm ready to tell you," I say and then take a few deep breaths.

"You remember back in high school, Chris, when I was always so quick to leave the locker room," I tell him.

"Yeah, I guess so. You always seemed to get dressed and get the hell out of there," he says with confusion in his voice.

"Yeah, well, there was a reason for that. I was terrified about being in there around all those naked guys."

"Um…terrified? Why would you be….ohhhh," he answers catching himself as he realizes what I'm saying.

"I'm sorry. I've wanted to tell you for awhile, but for some reason it never seemed to be the right time," I say trying to stay focused.

I look at him, my best friend for so many years. There seems to be some anger in his face and I'm not too sure what he's about to say, but I can feel the beads of sweat forming on my forehead.

"Are you telling me that all those times you rushed out of the locker room was because you were afraid you might get a boner?" he says starting to laugh a little.

"Yeah, I guess so. I can't believe you're laughing," I say slightly shocked.

"Sorry, I'm just trying to imagine you having to think of Margaret Thatcher on a cold day every time you found yourself in the locker room," he says with another laugh. "Hey, I'm all about live and let live or love. As long as you're happy, that's all that matters. I may not understand all of it and I probably won't want to hear all of your stories, but I really don't think this will change anything. You're my best friend."

He reaches over and gives me a guy hug and I start to tear up.

"Good lord, here come the tears," he says smiling ever so slightly. "Now why don't you tell me everything that happened tonight so I can help you?"

My shoulders, which have been so tense for the past few minutes, begin to relax slightly and I start to go into the details of the evening. Chris is attentive and gets pretty upset when I tell him about the hookup.

"You do realize that you're a fucking moron to have gone home with that guy right?" he says with a mixture of anger and concern.

"Wow, your support's really appreciated," I say with a somewhat surprised look.

"Don't give me that crap, Brad. I don't care how long you've been out of the closet and that you needed to get your rocks off, but come on! What that dick did to you is inexcusable, but your dumb ass should never have been there in the first place. And by the way, your mother and father would be extremely pissed if they knew you were getting drunk like that. Let me jog your memory, Brad. You almost died a while back. Why would you do something to put yourself in that position again just by drinking too much?" he asks incredulously.

This was truly not the reaction I expected after just coming out to him. He's actually angrier about everything else that happened than the fact that I'm gay.

"I know you're right, Chris. On a more positive side though, I've gone to the LGBT Center on campus and they're helping with a lot of the stuff that I'm dealing with," I say trying to steer the conversation into better territory.

"You know what, Brad; just do me a favor and don't do stupid shit like that again. I've enough to do without having to deal with you in the hospital all the time."

"Okay, okay, I promise. Boy, you sure sound like my mother, but then again she doesn't say shit quite that way," I say trying to lighten things up.

"Speaking of that, have you told them?"

"I think they have an idea, but no, I haven't specifically said anything yet."

"Well, don't wait too long. They really shouldn't be the last ones to know. They're your parents and you know they're going to understand."

"I know. It's just they're so far away and it's always felt like I need to do it face to face. But don't worry, Chris. I'll do it soon."

Chris is right of course. I need to have that conversation with my parents. I haven't even spoken to them in awhile. But, I'll deal with that when I get out of here.

"I'm gonna close my eyes for a few. If you wanna leave, I can give you a call when they say I can go home," I say starting to feel tired again.

"Now what kind of friend would I be leaving you here all by your lonesome? I grabbed a few things on the way out of the dorm and can watch some shows on my iPad. It's all good," he says as he plops down into the vinyl chair in the corner by a double window with blinds that are beginning to look really crooked in my blurry tired eyes.

This is why I was afraid to tell Chris I'm gay. I didn't want to lose all of this. Here he is literally willing to stay here all night by my side after all the ridiculous stuff I have just told him. I suppose it's like that song. You know the one about always remaining friends in both good times and bad. That really is what friends are for and I know that as I close my eyes. I'm in good hands with my best friend beside me.

After what seems like hours, I feel someone tapping on my shoulder. It's the nurse from earlier in the evening. I glance at the clock and hours have gone by. The sun is starting to come up.

"Hi, Mr. Archer. How are you feeling?" he asks as he leans over to check the IV drip

Looking at him, I make the cheesiest comment in the world, "Well looking at you makes me feel a whole lot better."

He smiles at me and gives me a wink possibly acknowledging that we are in the same club. I sure hope so. I can see Chris out of the corner of my eye rolling his eyes.

"I cannot believe I just heard you say that! I suppose this means that Mary's back on the table. I might just give her a call a little later," he says with a scheming smile.

"Well, I do need to get back to my initial question, Mr. Archer. Are you feeling well enough for me to remove the IV and start prepping you for release?" the nurse asks.

"Yeah, yeah. I'm starting to feel a lot better. My headache's mostly gone away, but my face is still a little sore under my eye and in fact I really need to pee."

"Why don't you take care of that while I get your paper work and sign off with your doctor?"

"Whoa!" I exclaim as I slide out of the bed and feel a sudden draft on my backside. Apparently when my pants were removed so was my underwear. The back of my gown isn't tied and I'm flapping in the breeze! I can hear whistling behind me. Chris is laughing and the nurse's smile seems to cover his whole face as I grab the gown shut and head to the bathroom, closing the door behind me.

In the bathroom I take a moment to look at myself in the mirror. I look exhausted and the bruising around my eye is a reminder of my stupidity last night. I take a quick look at my butt and even though it still hurts, it looks okay. Suddenly my mind jump starts to thoughts of the cute man getting ready to discharge me. Really, Brad, really! This is what you're thinking about right now? Remember all the shit that happened last night and keep things in perspective. Someone forced himself on you. You were basically raped. This is absolutely not the time to be thinking about sex with someone you just met. Use the head above your shoulders, Brad. Come on!

Before leaving the bathroom, I reach behind me and tie the gown tightly. Closing the door, I see Chris standing right there in front of me. He has a small grin on his face and then he does the unexpected. He opens his arms and gives me a huge hug and it's surprisingly longer than I would've expected from him.

"Whoa, that's not what I expected," I say as I step back from my best friend.

"Listen, it means a lot to me that you told me. You know, Brad, you could've come to me sooner when you were struggling," he says.

"I know that now, but there's a reason for that…," I trail off from my sentence trying to find the right words.

"It's okay. You're allowed to keep things to yourself. I really don't mind," he says, but I can tell he's disappointed that I haven't told him everything.

Chris has even thought to bring some of his clothes that I can wear home. He must have thought I wouldn't want to wear the ones I was in last night. I take them from him and start to dress, slipping on the underwear under my hospital gown.

"You've always been my closest friend, Chris. You're the person I have always felt safe with. I always knew you had my back no matter what," I pause and look closely at Chris. "I honestly don't know where I'd be without you. I think because of all of that I've…I've…well… I've been attracted to you too. I know, I know, you're straight and don't have any reciprocal feelings, but that doesn't change the fact that I have them. In time I know I'll meet someone, but during all of this, it's been tough knowing that the person I care for the most outside of my parents is out of reach." Stopping, I gulp before finishing. "I just don't want the fact that I told you this to change our friendship," I say so worried about his response.

There's a tear in Chris's eye. Something I never expected since he has never really shown all that much emotion around me before.

"I get it, Brad, and it really means a lot to me. I know you could've gone your whole life without telling me because you were afraid that it would distance us or end our friendship," he says.

"I have to say that did cross my mind."

"Well, I think it's time for you to uncross it, buddy. You're my best friend and you always will be. Gay or straight doesn't factor into our friendship at all for me, but the fact that you've told me your feelings means a lot. You opened up to me. Okay, based on the circumstances maybe those weren't the best words to use, but I really hope this makes us even closer friends. I would appreciate it though if you wouldn't put the moves on me all the time," he continues with a smile. "God, this is great! I can attract the ladies and the men. I really should wake up every morning and thank God for this beautiful specimen of a body."

I smile at him wondering if there will ever be a time when I can be more like him. Confident. Happy. I also hope they'll be a time when I can see Chris and not have the sexual yearnings I've fought for years. But at least I know he understands.

Buttoning up my shirt, I start gathering my cell phone and wallet and keycard to my dorm as the doctor walks into the room. He's in his early 40s with a trim build, black hair and wearing dark framed glasses."

"Mr. Archer? My name is Dr. Hamilton. Your nurse seems to think you're ready for check out. How are you feeling young man?"

"I'm feeling much better. I have a little headache still, but nothing like before."

"You may not remember this, but we ran an MRI and you did suffer a mild concussion which may cause you to have headaches for the next few days. If the headaches start to get worse, you have any dizziness or have trouble remembering, I need you to call the hospital immediately. The most important thing is to make sure to rest and take care of yourself. I don't know all of the details but whatever confrontation you were in, you need to resolve that and avoid that kind of stress. It's not good for your head or your diabetes. And do me a favor, Mr. Archer, don't drink. Feel free to use Tylenol for the headaches. You can take up to three every four hours. Please remember to rest. This was a very traumatic experience and you need to take care of yourself," the doctor says with authority.

"Don't worry, doctor. I'll be sure he takes care of himself," Chris interjects.

The doctor goes over a few more checks with my vision and may head. "Okay, then, I've signed your forms, Mr. Archer, and you're ready to go. My phone number is at the bottom of the discharge form and remember, call if anything concerns you. You have a follow-up appointment next week. Now is this young man who's taking you home planning on staying with you for at least the next 24 hours?

"Yes, doctor," Chris says. "I'll be driving him back to school and will stay with him today."

"Good. Good. Now here's your paperwork. Dylan will wheel chair you out of here."

"Oh, I'm fine, Doctor, I don't need a wheelchair," I protest.

"Company policy, young man. Take care," he says extending his hand.

I shake his hand and wait as Dylan comes in with the wheel chair. I slowly walk over to the chair with Chris' guidance and suddenly get a wave of dizziness as I sort of fall into the chair.

"Whoa there, big boy, there's no need to rush. You got all your stuff?" Dylan asks.

"Yeah, I'm all set," I say as the three of us head for the exit. It takes a few minutes to get to the parking garage as it's on the opposite side of the building. During the trek, Chris, who has apparently become my dating service, does some investigating to find out a little more about Dylan who is starting med school next year.

"I mean I know it sounds corny, but I've always wanted to help people. I started out as a nurse, but then decided I wanted to go all the way and become a doctor," he says with a smile. "I'm doing a rotation with Doctor Hamilton this semester and sometimes I get lucky and get really cute patients," he says smiling even wider.

Chris nudges me and asks, "So did you get lucky today?"

"Yeah, I'd say today is one of the luckier days I've had in a while."

"I think Brad feels the same way," Chris says.

Embarrassed I throw Chris a look to kill. Once we're at Chris' car, Dylan reminds Chris to go to the pharmacy before we get to the dorm because I'll probably need the Tylenol before I get home. I thank him once again and shake his hand.

As he hands me the forms he says, "If you need anything at all, please feel free to let me know. Take care, Brad. I'm sure you'll be fine."

As he walks back into the hospital, I look at the forms and sigh, wishing I had gotten his number. I mean who knows what could've happened. Reading over the forms in the car, I drop one of them and notice that Dylan's written his name and number on the back of the form. Under them it says, *I probably shouldn't be giving you this, but you seem like a really sweet guy. Give me a call some time. Dylan.*

I keep rereading the note and smile. His number is listed right after his name. Yes! I turn to Chris and thank him again for everything he's done.

"Hey, man, no problem. I do have one question though."

"Shoot."

"Why did it take you so long to come out? I mean you must have known your parents and Laura and I weren't going to have any issues with it and most likely the rest of the gang was going to be okay too."

I start to respond quickly but I reconsider and take a few seconds to think about the best way to tell him.

"I guess a lot of it has to do with the way society views homosexuality. That's really bothered me this whole time. I mean look at Russia and how they treat gay people there. And I've just always felt it was wrong for me. You know I've never had any issues with gay people. It's *me* being gay that bothered me the most," I stop and hesitate for a moment. "I'm planning on telling my parents, Chris, in the next couple of days. I need to," I say convincing myself as much as telling him.

"Well you better tell them soon, Brad. Like I said before, it'd be bad if they found out from someone else. I do get your feelings on being gay. With all the crazies out there it can be tough knowing you're something that a bunch of people hate. But, god, it's gotten so much better in the last few years. You gotta remember that," he says optimistically.

"You're right. I'm gonna tell my parents. Just another part of my laundry list of things I really need to do."

I do really need to tell them. Last summer they told me it was okay to be gay. Now I just have to tell them that I know I am.

12

"Divinely bent to meditation"

Over the next two days I do my best to relax. It's time to get better and get back to focusing on my classes. I finally have a strong idea for my film and if it comes to fruition I think it could be great, but I've got to sketch out a plan, and soon.

Although it's been great staying with Chris for the past two days, I do need to get back to my room. I've got to get my stuff I need. I spoke with my R.A. and he and the administrator of the dorm spoke with Jonathan and it seems, for now at least, he's moved off campus. I told them I was concerned about my belongings and they assured me that if he took anything there would be even worse consequences for him. I hope he's not so stupid to take or destroy anything else. They also informed me that I have an appointment with the dean of residence tomorrow morning to discuss the situation. I'm not totally sure whether I'm happy about this or not, but if it can help bring a resolution to my roommate situation then so be it. I guess I'll also have to deal with the fact that I probably broke a dozen rules in the student hand book with my display of Jonathan's underwear. Still, what I did made me feel better and right now I don't regret it.

After grabbing some breakfast with Laura and Chris, I decide to head over to my room and assess the damage. I've really got to get the rest of my important things out of there. I have no idea where they're going to put me or when that's gonna happen, but I do need stuff for class and clothes for the rest of the week. Right now, needless to say, I'm feeling pretty displaced.

Standing in front of my door, I immediately flashback to everything in my room covered with the word FAGGOT and equally hateful words. It's like those flashbacks you see in movies or on *Dexter*. I see Jonathan's fist coming at my face. I take a moment, lean against the wall and breathe slowly until I'm calm enough to slide my card and enter the room.

It's like a crime scene where people have come in and cleaned up everything. Jonathan's stuff is completely gone and all the writing and notes have disappeared. My clothes are all put away as well, which seems really weird. Who'd take all my stuff and put it away for me?

"Um, yup, we did that," I hear Laura say from behind me.

"We thought it would be best if you came back to a room that was a little more Brad friendly," she says giving me a big smile as she and Chris walk into the room. "The R.A. let us in earlier," says Laura.

I smile at the both of them and give each of them a hug.

"I really appreciate it, guys, but you didn't have to go to all that trouble. You know I kinda wish you hadn't seen all that stuff on the wall."

Chris nods his head and says, "Hey, dude, it's not like we haven't heard or seen those words before and you're our friend. This is what we do. Oh and by the way, this means whenever I need a helping hand, you'll have to be there for me. Right?" he says with a wink and light punch to my shoulder.

"Come on. I'm always gonna be there for you, both of you. I don't know where I'd be without you."

As I start to pick up my things, Chris and Laura do the same, putting my stuff in boxes they'd brought in earlier. Feeling light headed, I sit for a moment on my bed and test my blood sugar. It's 54. That's not good. I head over to the small fridge in the room and grab a bottle of apple juice and drink it down quickly.

"Hey, guys, you mind if I take a short break?" I ask lying down on the bed.

"Typical Brad, using your diabetes as a crutch to get out of work. When I need a break, I have to admit I'm just lazy and tired," Chris says laughing and this time Laura gives him a punch in the arm.

Lying on my bed, I close my eyes thinking about everything that has happened. Suddenly I have flashes of Harvey Bobson trying to kiss me merging with images of my roommate writing those obscenities everywhere and Bobby forcing himself on me. Everything starts flooding back at once and the anxiety begins to overwhelm me. I hyperventilate and have what I can only describe as a genuine "freak out".

Quickly Laura moves over to me and rubs my back and shoulders.

"Brad, try and relax. It's going to be okay. Now breathe slowly. That's it, in and out."

"No, it isn't, Laura! No it isn't! This is too much! I have to tell people what happened, I have to get my projects done for school and who knows, the administration might kick me out for what I did to retaliate. What am I going to do, guys? I mean seriously. What am I going to do?" I cry.

Chris moves over to me and grabs my face forcing me to face him.

"Here's what you are going to do, Brad. You're going to trust that your friends are going to help you through this. We know it's hard, but you have to try and get a grip. It's gonna be okay. Right now you just need to take some more deep breaths."

Slowly I begin to calm down. I guess being in this room and knowing what Jonathan did to it was more than I could handle. Not to mention my encounter with that asshole Bobby and what he did to me. After a few minutes I start to feel better and we pack up the rest of my stuff and head to the elevator and down to Chris' car, which is parked out front. We stuff all of my things in the back seat and trunk.

"I know I sound like a broken record, but I can't thank you guys enough for helping me. This wasn't easy but with you helping it was bearable," I say.

"No problem, my man. You know what, let's invite some people over to my place. My roommates are gone and we can sit back and relax for a bit," Chris says.

"Yeah, I suppose I could use a little diversion and I don't have that much work to do for tomorrow. But I do need to try to work a little on my film, that's if I can concentrate enough," I reply with a small sigh.

Back at Chris' place he let's me use his room and after an hour or so working on the outline for my film, I walk back into the living area to see five of my friends sitting on the couches relaxing. The scent of marijuana is a bit overwhelming, but welcoming none the less. I'm sure not what anyone would call a pothead, but there are those moments when it relaxes me enough to stop worrying nonstop about my life. First I test my blood, 143, perfect. I'm not sure I should be doing this considering everything I've been through, but I need to relax and forget about the shit that's my life at the moment.

Whoa…this is exactly what I needed. I'm pretty baked right now. We're all sitting here watching *Willy Wonka and the Chocolate Factory* and it's pretty messed up. I've seen the movie dozens of times, but never like this before.

As I drift into my high, my mind starts to relax even more although the movie is freaking me out to some degree. That scene on the boat in the tunnel is crazy. Suddenly I start thinking about stuff I've never considered before.

"Hey, guys, do you mind if we just talk for a sec?" I ask tentatively.

They all take their eyes off the TV and turn to me as the movie stops abruptly. The room is filled with five of my good friends Jeff, Sarah, Jake, Laura and Chris and before I went in to finish my studies, I had told them my coming out story.

"So guys, I...um wanted to tell you...um. I'm gay," I said tentatively.

"That's cool," Jake said. "Yup, no problem here", Jeff echoed.

Sarah even added, "That's awesome. We need to go shopping."

"Well that was easier than I thought it would be," I said completely surprised.

"Brad, we all watch *Glee* and *Modern Family.* It's all good," Jeff said with a smile.

It was great to be able to tell a bunch of them all at once and it was easy. If I had told everyone separately and took them out for food, the last of them would be having Happy Meals. Hey, I'm a college kid on a limited budget.

Back in my semi-stoned stupor I say, "So everyone I have a really important question that I need an honest answer for."

"Yeah. Sure. Of course," echo the group.

"Do you think Bert and Ernie are a happy gay couple? I mean they seem to argue all the time and Bert never seems to be really happy with Ernie," I propose to the group.

With a hazy smile Chris and puts his arm around my shoulder and says, "Brad, they do take a lot of baths together. That has to count for something."

Everyone laughs and so do I. God, I never thought it was going to go like this. This feels great. I can't believe I can say I feel great, but I do. I mean I literally got drunk, was basically raped by a stranger and then knocked out by my roommate. Holy shit that is a lot, but somehow all the hor-ridness seems just a little less – a little further in the past. I try to blank Bobby and Jonathan out of my mind as we talk about watching Sesame Street and how much we loved it as kids, and before we know it, we've moved on to Mr. Rogers, all tossing our shoes in the air like Fred Rogers. At least he could catch his while the rest of us hit ourselves in the head or lose the shoes under the couches.

Suddenly I feel myself fading. "You know what guys, I'm going to bed. Thanks for everything," I say.

They say goodnight and I head to the bathroom where I wash my face, floss and brush my teeth. Then I look into the mirror.

"I'm gay and it's okay," I say to my reflection. I pull on my pajama pants, actually the ones with Bert and Ernie on them, and a raggy, but comfortable tee shirt and lie down on the inflatable mattress on the floor of Chris' room. I know tomorrow's going to be a crazy day. Meeting with the dean is going to be stressful. I should probably call Kevin and apolo-gize too. I haven't checked my phone intentionally because right now I just can't deal with any of that. As I plug the phone into the charger though, I notice there are five texts and two missed calls from Kevin and one from my parents. Crap, I was supposed to call them this weekend and check in. Depending on how the meeting goes with the dean, I might have to tell them a lot more than I want. I'll just wait and call them after my meeting with the dean.

For now I try my best to clear my mind. No Harvey Bobson, no Jonathan, no Bobby – just good thoughts. Usually before I fall asleep I imagine something I really like, whether it be a movie or T.V. show I love, or even a memory from when I was a kid. Sometimes this helps me avoid the nightmares that come far too often. The memory I conjure up tonight is one when I was a kid and we used to go to my grandparents' house up on Sebago Lake in Maine. I always had so much fun up there. Since I didn't have a brother all that long, it was always great to see my cousins and aunts and uncles. They're great family and those summers were always filled with lots of laughter, great times swimming in the lake and excellent sandwiches made by my grandmother. As I close my eyes, I imagine sitting at the table on the deck surrounded by my extended family. My mom and dad are smiling and chatting with my uncle. As the sun beats down on my face, I take a bite out of my sandwich and think, this is the life. I slowly drift off to sleep remembering a time when there were little to no cares in the world and swimming in a crystal clear lake was as good as it gets.

13

"Woe to the hand that shed this costly blood!"

After what seems to be an extremely long deep sleep, I stretch my arms and rub my eyes trying to get some focus to the morning. A quick glance at my insulin pump, shows me my numbers are in range, but I test my blood regardless. Today's not a day to play games with my numbers. One thirty five. Great. Looking over to the alarm clock, I wonder why I woke up before it went off. Oh no... oh no...this isn't good. Apparently in the haze that was last night, I forgot I'd left my alarm clock along with most of my stuff out in the main living area. I have a 10:15 meeting with Dean Russell and was sternly warned by his secretary that I best be on time. Shit, it's 9:40.

Happily everyone else is either still asleep or in class already. I take one of the quickest showers of my life and rifle through my clothes trying to find a button-down shirt that's not too wrinkled – not an easy task for someone who grabbed all of his clothes and shoved them into any box or suitcase available 15 hours ago. After five minutes of searching, I can't find anything presentable. Quickly I sneak back into Chris' room. He's sound asleep. I go through his closet and find a shirt that not only fits but isn't even wrinkled. I take a look in the mirror, give myself a quick nod of approval, followed by a deep breath and head out the door.

At least the dean's office is not too far from Chris' on campus apartment (lucky son of a gun he was to get one) and it only takes me five minutes to get over there. It's a beautiful day. Maybe that's a good omen for what's ahead.

Standing outside Dean Russell's office, I'm reminded of when I used to walk past the principal's office in high school and see kids waiting for their punishment. I'm not sure what or if there will be any punishment for this fiasco, but I've decided that whatever happens, I'll deal with it and move on – at least that's what I'm telling myself as I open the door.

"He's ready for you, Mr. Archer," says the middle-aged secretary, who is wearing what I can only describe as librarian glasses and the brightest blue suit I've ever seen, as she points to the door on the other side of the office.

I take a moment to make sure my shirt is tucked in and push back my hair. I rub my hands together a few times, stand up straighter, throw my shoulders back and make my way into Dean Russell's office. His office is much like any other administrator's on campus. He has a large mahogany desk and a hell of a lot of file cabinets. A flat screen TV is mounted on a wall across from his desk. The T.V., muted, is on the campus station and seems to be playing a repeat of the morning news. I'm impressed that he's watching it. At least it shows he's interested in what's happening on campus. There are what appear to be dozens of papers strewn across the desk. I'm sure there's some organization to it all, but it's certainly hard to tell.

"Please have a seat, Mr. Archer," Dean Russell says with a commanding voice as he looks up from the papers in front of him.

"Thank you, sir," I reply with obvious nervousness in my voice.

"As you know, young man, we are here to discuss the incident that occurred this past Saturday in your dormitory," he says looking me straight in the eye.

"Yes, sir," I answer starting to feel even more uneasy.

"Let us start with the facts and please feel free to explain if any of my information is incorrect. I apologize that you are going to have to relive some of this, but it really is the only way. Do you understand, Mr. Archer?"

I nod quickly. I just want to get this over with and find out what's going to happen.

"Now, you came into your dormitory during the day to find that your room had been vandalized with homophobic slurs written on the wall and on your possessions. Also many of your possessions, including clothing, were destroyed. At this point, your roommate was not present in the room. Is this all correct?"

"Yes sir. That is correct."

"In retribution for what your roommate did, you decided to take his undergarments and tape them to the wall of the hallway outside of your room while also placing a notice that they were free for the taking."

"Yes, sir," I mumble, hanging my head a little as I remember the scene oh so well.

"It was when you returned later that evening that your roommate, Mr. Brandson, engaged in a violent altercation with you. As you opened the door to walk in, he surprised you with a punch to the face and you subsequently fell backward and hit your head against the wall knocking you out."

"As far as I know, that is correct, sir."

"Well, now that we have all the facts out there, let's discuss why this incident occurred. First and foremost, as you may know, Mr. Archer, this university has a zero tolerance level when it comes to discrimination and any verbal, written or physical abuse that comes from that discrimination. Now I'm not here to ask you anything personal, son. You're...."

"Sir?" I ask sensing he's uncomfortable with part of the conversation.

"Yes, Mr. Archer," replies Dean Russell as he leans forward in his chair.

"I'm gay, sir. I know you feel you can't ask that question so I'm going to put it out there right now. It's taken me a long time to figure it out, but I am. When my roommate found out, it had literally only been a short time since I had come to terms with who I am."

"I do appreciate you sharing that information, Mr. Archer. I'm sure it hasn't been easy to have to once again open up about all of this. Your sexuality to some degree is irrelevant. Whether you are or are not gay does not in any way excuse Mr. Brandson's behavior."

"I understand, sir."

"After meeting with other administrators, it has been determined that Mr. Brandson will no longer be attending this university. His actions do not align with the philosophy of this institution or the behavior we expect and demand from our students."

For the first time since walking into his office, my shoulders begin relax a little. The fact that I won't have to be constantly looking out for Jonathan lurking somewhere, trying in any way possible to make my life miserable, makes me extremely happy.

"If you decide to file charges against Mr. Brandson, you are certainly within your rights to do so. Since this altercation happened on campus, Mr. Archer, the university would be a part of any of those proceedings."

I look up slightly startled. I hadn't even considered the notion of filing charges against Jonathan. Doing that would mean I'd have to spend more time dealing with him and I know I don't want to do that. Expulsion fits the crime here and I tell Dean Russell exactly that.

"There is, however, one more issue that we need to deal with," replies Dean Russell, looking up at me with an especially stern look.

"The matter of vandalism and assault against you has been dealt with, but the way you responded is still a matter that must be addressed. As you are aware, there are many ways of handling difficult situations. Very often emotions dictate our reactions and this is not always the best case."

"I understand sir, and mine most certainly wasn't," I reply, waiting for the shoe to drop.

"Your emotional reaction was not the right choice. What you should have done was notify your dorm representative and he would have notified campus police and it would have been handled quickly. Instead you made a rash decision which in turn provoked your roommate to react the way he did."

Dean Russell then does something I find to be uncharacteristic for a person who is dressing me down. He gets out of his chair, comes around the desk and sits in the chair next to me. He turns the chair, faces me and puts his hand on my shoulder.

"Listen, son, I have kids of my own and I've been doing this job for a long time. I do understand what all of this must be like for you. I hear that you've met with George Martens and he said you and he have had some good discussions. He left it at that as they are *your* discussions. There are, however, consequences for the things you do. Understand that I will not be putting this in your permanent record, but you will have to do some volunteering here at the university. Since you are meeting with George, I'm going to wave the requirement to meet with a counselor. I do, however, expect you to have a discussion with George concerning your behavior with this incident. Again, I must state that although what happened to you was uncalled for, your reaction was as well. There's no three strike policy here. I hope this is the only time we will ever meet to discuss this. If I have you back here, again, I will be very disappointed, Mr. Archer," he says straightening up in his chair.

"I promise, sir. This has been a learning lesson and you will not be seeing me again," I reply quickly.

"There's an old saying I tell people who are having a rough time...'this too shall pass'. And it will, Mr. Archer. Trust me. It will. Things will get better and know that most people are not like your former roommate. Now my secretary, Madeline, will get you squared away with the people you will need to talk to about getting a new room assignment. She will also give you the forms for your volunteering requirement. Know that I'm pulling for you to have a single room, but we'll have to see what's available."

"Thank you, Dean Russell. I really do appreciate all of this and I promise to remember what you said."

"See that you do, young man."

Smiling he gets out of the chair, straightens his navy blazer, and extends his hand. As I reach out to shake his hand, he places his other hand on my shoulder and gives me a quick look of encouragement. I leave the office totally relieved.

I spend the next fifteen minutes or so with his secretary and get all the contact information I need for my new room assignment. I also have a list of options for volunteering. I'm actually looking forward to this. I've always enjoyed helping others.

Leaving the building, I find a bench near the campus convenience store and sit down. My next class isn't till eleven so I have a few minutes to settle my mind and body. Deciding I should get a quick snack, I head into the convenience store and grab a Diet Coke and Cheez Its. Outside I sit down and take a long slug of soda. A sharp pain starts radiating in the back of my head. Fumbling through my bag I find the bottle of Tylenol and pop three in my mouth. There's no way I can get through class with a headache like the one I've got right now.

Suddenly I feel a hand placed on my shoulder. Startled, I turn and see Kevin standing over me. He has a small smile on his face which instantly makes me feel a little better.

"Well...well...well," he says, his voice laced with playfulness

I stand up and suddenly start to feel a little dizzy. I immediately sit back down, my body rocking back and forth as I rub my temples. Kevin quickly moves and sits beside me. Even with my head pounding, my brain registers that he looks good in a Marc Jacobs shirt and a pair of jeans that are really slim and seem to show off his butt as he plants it down on the bench.

"Whoa, easy there, cowboy. There's no reason to get up," he says as he puts his hand on my shoulder and eases me back down on the bench.

"Damn. It's been a really crazy last few days."

"I bet, but a little stress on your side doesn't excuse you for not returning any of my calls or texts. Man, I was *really* worried about you. I mean you left so quick. I couldn't find you anywhere. I went searching all the neighboring bars for you. Thank god I was able to find the last name of your friend Chris through a friend on campus and I gave him a call to check up on you," he says.

"Yeah, I'm sorry about that, Kevin. That was a pretty shitty thing to do."

"Yeah, it was, but I'm glad you're okay and out of the hospital. What the hell were you thinking? Your friend didn't really give me the details outside of what your roommate did to you. I'm afraid I told George what happened. I think I needed to do that, Brad. I believe he spoke with one of the deans on your behalf."

"Well that makes a lot of sense. I guess that's why Dean Russell was so kind to me when I met with him earlier this morning. I'll have to thank George for defending me. You know I thought I'd be upset about someone revealing things about me, but I guess if it helped me get a better reaction from administration, then it's all good," I answer now having a better insight into this morning meeting.

Kevin suggests we walk over to the Student Center where there's a little more privacy so we can talk some more. I can sense he really needs to know what happened. Sitting down in a quiet corner, I start to explain how and why I left the bar and then my encounter with Bobby.

"I don't think you'll want to rank that one in your top ten experiences with a man," Kevin says with a shake of his head.

"Someone once told me that the first person you're with should be a boyfriend. That's all well and good, but most often our hormones get the better of us and we end up fucking someone we really don't know. And you know what, Brad; it usually doesn't end up being what we want."

"I really do regret it. I was angry about something that in the end I really shouldn't have been. You gave me no indications you were interested in me that way. I guess I just misread the whole dynamic. I mean you were the first gay person to ever reach out to me and I just had unrealistic expectations. In the end I found the outlet I thought I wanted only to find that making a connection with someone is a hell of a lot more important than just a dick and two balls. That and the fact that I was also drunk out of my mind," I say somberly. "I guess I can be a real idiot sometimes."

"One thing I try to avoid, Brad, is blaming my actions on anything but myself. It's always easy to say that it was the booze or something else, but in the end you make a decision for something you think you want at the time. You're not going to like this part, Brad, but you're probably going to make more missteps when it comes to hooking up with people. That's just the nature of it," says Kevin.

"In a way, all I want is for things to be back the way they were when I wasn't worrying all the time. It seems like I've come a long way so far, Kevin, but I still feel like it's gonna keep going like this with no end in sight. Can you begin to understand what I mean?"

Kevin looks at me and smiles before saying, "Of course it feels that way, Brad. You've had some shitty experiences with coming out, but you've also had some great ones. Hold on to the good ones. That's what I did. All of this craziness will come to an end. You'll tell the people you love and maybe a few others and that will be it. Just remember there are so many things that make you who you are. You're a kind, loving person, Brad, who loves film, is a diabetic and happens to be gay. All of those things are part of what makes you the person you are. No single one has to be more important than another. You know, Brad, there are a lot of people out there that allow the fact that they're gay to define them. You can choose to do that or you can make your sexuality a part of the whole. That's what I do. I think it'll work for you too," he says.

"It just feels like I have so much more work to do," I answer in anything but an upbeat voice.

Kevin laughs and squeezes my hand. "Ain't life a bitch, but this is life, my friend, and to put it bluntly, you're just gonna have to live with it. Now listen, Brad, you really need to stop thinking negatively and concentrate on doing the things that make you happy."

"Tough love, huh." I say with a small smile.

"Yup. Well, I gotta get to class. I'm glad I saw you today. I really was worried, Brad. Just do me a favor. When you walk out of the bar next time, make sure you leave enough money for the tab," he says with a quick wink.

"I thought; well, I meant…" I stammer.

"Relax. Just kidding. Remember we're friends and I want it to stay that way. Call me and we can go out again. Hey, and make sure you talk to George too. He can do an awful lot for you. He's a good guy and he's helped a lot of people."

"I will," I tell him. "And thanks, Kevin. I really do appreciate everything."

Getting up off the couch, I still feel slightly woozy, but okay enough to head to class. Here's hoping I can take good enough notes so I can read them when mid terms come around. It really is time to set aside the gay stuff for a bit. Three classes to get through and then there's a call I've needed to make for a long time – the one to mom and dad.

14

"Thou canst not then be false to any man" (parent)

It's time for me to head over to the Residence Center where Dean Russell's secretary told me I would find information concerning my dorm situation. I know I can stay with Chris for as long as I need, but I do need to have my own space.

It takes almost an hour to get through the entire process, but overall it's easier than I thought. The people are nice and understand that I've been through a lot with Jonathan. Apparently this is not a totally unique situation. Seems there are quite a few crappy roommates out there. Considering the potency of the issues though, they decide to grant me a single in the same dorm. Throughout the conversations it seemed they actually knew very few specifics of my case – just that it was really bad. Thank god. I'm not sure I want that many people knowing what I went through. This is by far the best outcome I could have hoped for. I really like most of the people in my dorm and being able to stay there will bring more stability to my life. Most of them also know I'm a diabetic and will check in on me if they don't see me around. The counselors at the Residence Center informed me I can move in this evening. This is a sign of good things to come. I can feel it.

Speaking of stabilizing my life, there's still something major I need to do. My parents have called a couple times over the last few days and I need to get back to them. They're 3,000 miles away and there is no way I can get away from school to head east right now. I've arranged to chat with them via Facetime since we both have iPads. I know I have to be able to see them when I tell them.

One of the things I'm concerned about is the family line. With the death of my brother and the fact that my dad only has sisters, I'm the only one who can carry on the Archer line. I hadn't really thought about it all that much until right now. Being gay sort of takes me out of the equation of having my own kid. I mean I know there are some gay couples that have kids through surrogates, but I'm pretty sure that's not gonna happen for me. This is just another sucky part to being gay. I just don't want to disappoint my dad given the fact that I might not give him a grandkid.

Pulling my iPad out of my backpack, I get it ready. Both my parents should be home from work now and not have started dinner yet.

As it seems to be with everything I do right now, I take a few deep breaths and then enter the digits on the house phone to call them first to set up Facetime.

"Hi, Brad," answers my mom with enthusiasm in her voice.

"Hi, Mom. How are you?" I ask tentatively.

"Things are good here, honey. It's been a while since we've been able to chat. We miss you, Brad. Both Dad and I have left you a couple of messages. Is everything okay?"

"Can we Facetime now, Mom? It's actually really comforting to see your faces," I say feigning confidence I don't really have at the moment.

"Sure, Brad," she replies. "I'll call you, hon."

We hang up and I wait a few moments for the ring on the iPad. It rings and I hit the connect button.

"Hi, Mom. Hi, Dad. I haven't gotten back to you because there's just been a lot going on here with classes and some other stuff. I've kind of had some issues with my roommate over the past few days."

"Are you okay, Brad? He didn't do anything bad to you did he?" my mom asks with obvious concern in her voice. I can see the anger rise in my dad's eyes.

"Well, I thought it would be better for me to tell you in person, but there's no way I can do that. So here I am. Jonathan and I had some issues and the school stepped in and I have a single now in the same dorm. So everything's pretty much settled for the best."

"Brad, what happened? Why did you to have to change rooms? You're making me nervous, hon," my mom says anxiously.

I get cold feet and take a very quick moment to decide whether I'm going to tell them now or I wait until I see them in a few months at the end of the year.

Before I called home I took some time to think about my parents. I've been doing that a lot over the last few days. When you're a kid you never really think of all the little things they do for you. I mean at the time it's really just something you expect from them because they're your parents. But recently two stories keep running through my head. When I was diagnosed with diabetes, I was completely unaware of the disease and what it meant. Even after all the educational training I had to go through, I was still nervous all the time. I know – big surprise that I was nervous. I remember each morning before I took a shower and got ready for school, or work on weekends, I would go downstairs to the kitchen. My mom would have my insulin in a syringe ready to go. I would sit, blurry eyed, like any teenager at that time, and she would give me my first shot of the day. She never said a thing about doing this. It was just something she felt she had to do to make my days a little easier. I never thought till now how amazing that was of her.

I also remember late spring afternoons with my dad. I would get all my homework done early so I would be ready to throw a baseball around with him when he got home. I never considered the fact he had over an hour commute each way to work and must have been exhausted when he got home. I'm sure throwing a baseball around was the last thing in the world he really wanted to do on some of those days, but he did it anyway. He would change into jeans and a tee shirt and we would "discuss our day". It usually meant me telling him all the things I did. I'm not sure if I ever really asked him about his day. Maybe this is something I can start doing now.

As my dad leans in closer to the iPad he says, "It's good to see you, Brad, but what happened to your eye? It looks black and blue."

"It's okay, dad. It was all part of the roommate thing, but it's fine now, honest," I say while slightly averting my eyes from his gaze.

"Honey, we're really concerned with the bruises. Please just tell us. You know I'll worry if you don't," my mom says and I know she's right. She always gets an A+ in the worry department.

"It's really okay. Jonathan and I got into an argument and he ended up hitting me in the face. I spoke with one of the deans and I'm being given a new room and he's been kicked out of Anderson."

"What prompted you to get into a fight with anyone, son? I mean I'd like to think we taught you better than to get into a fist fight with somebody," asks my dad.

I look at the two of them and know that this is the right thing to do. Suddenly a line from Shakespeare jumps into my head. I remember Ms. Mitchell in junior English spending so much time talking about the importance of being authentic to one's self and assigning journal entries based on the line "thou canst not then be false to any man."

"Well," I say slowly, trying to buy more time for myself. "We got into a fight because while I was out of the room, he wrote some pretty bad stuff all over my things."

"What are you talking about, Brad? Why would he do something like that, honey? What did he write?" my mother questions with rising concern.

Okay, Brad. I tell myself. Take a breath. "Faggot, mom. That's the word he wrote. He must have seen me going to the LGBT Center on campus and put two and two together and didn't like having a roommate like me."

My dad is clenching his fists. My mom's eyes are tearing up. I can't believe what I'm seeing. I really didn't expect them to react this way. "I'm so sorry, Mom and Dad. I don't want you to be mad or upset because I'm gay. I had to tell you this because it's who I am. I'm…I'm…still the same son…."

Quickly my mom interrupts and says, "We aren't mad that you're gay, honey. We've questioned that for awhile. We've just been waiting for you to tell us. We're upset that your roommate did what he did to you. You don't ever deserve to be treated in that manner. No one does," my mom continues, no longer trying to control her tears.

I breathe a sigh of relief, glad this hadn't gone in another direction.

"We love you, son", interrupts my dad. "It may not be the easiest thing to hear that your kid's gay, but believe me, we are okay with it and your happiness is all we truly want. Damn, I'm just so upset with your fucking roommate's behavior. Sorry, honey," he says turning to my mother and taking her hand.

"Dad, I'm really not sure at all why he's such as ass, but I don't have to worry about any of that now. He's gone and frankly, I don't give a damn why he thinks the way he does. As long as he's out of my life, I can go on with mine," I say with a newfound confidence grounded in their obvious approval of me.

"That's an extremely mature way to think about it, Brad, and I'm very proud of you for dealing with all of this on your own," my father replies.

"Well, I didn't do it all by myself, Dad. Laura and Chris have really been great through it all. "

"Having them as friends has always been so good for you, Brad. Thank god you have them in your life," my mom says smiling now.

Suddenly I decide it's time to explain a little more of how I came to this place in my life. "You remember last spring with all the Harvey Bobson stuff that went on?" I ask knowing damn well they'll never forget that incident.

"Of course. We tried to move him out of our minds as best we could, but someone like him and what he did to you will probably stay with us forever," my mom says and I know she has never forgotten that day.

"At least he's rotting in jail now, son. I was so happy they took care of him so he didn't do anything to anyone else," my dad says growling.

"This really isn't about him," I hesitate. "But more about the stuff afterwards. It's taken me time to think all this through and figure out who I am. I'm also so sorry this is the way we're doing this, Mom and Dad. I never expected to tell you on Facetime."

"Honey, this is what works now and, Brad, I'm just so glad I get to see your face even though it is so far away," my mother says, her voice catching with emotion.

"So I think I've known I'm gay for a long time, but I've finally come to the realization that this is who I am and maybe more importantly, I'm starting to be proud of being gay. For a long time I wasn't at all happy with this, but you know, once I realized I can't do anything to change it, I started slowly to accept that it's a part of who I am. I'm still in the very early stages of all of this, but I wanted you to know now."

My mom and dad each take each other's hands, squeeze them tightly and smile at me. It seems this has been rehearsed as they look at each other and nod.

"We've been prepared to talk to you about this for a long time. We've wondered," my mom explains looking directly at the iPad.

"We were told that it was best not to force anything on you, so we've waited for you to come to us. We tried not to assume anything, but we also wanted to be ready if in fact this day came. We even went to a few PFLAG meetings so we could learn how to be as supportive as possible," my mom explains.

Wow! I suppose it's true what they say about parents and the fact that they can always surprise you. The fact they went to a PFLAG meeting to try and be the best parents they could be to a son who may or may not be gay says so much of them as parents.

"That really means a lot to me. I can't believe you took all that time not even knowing one way or another," I say trying to control all the emotions I'm feeling right now.

My dad quickly adds, "The time didn't matter, son. It wasn't wasted. We've always tried to be the best parents we can be and part of that was being prepared for this day, if in fact it did happen. You know we love you, Brad, whether you're straight or not. It doesn't matter. We love you."

"Honey," adds my mom her voice once again filled with concern. "The thing that really bothers us is that we never wanted you to have to deal with issues like the one with your roommate. It's bad enough that you have diabetes, but now we know being gay is another issue you have to deal with. All we want is for you to be happy, Brad."

"I wasn't happy for a long time, Mom, but I'm starting to be now. I've gone to the Center on campus and met a few people and they've been extremely helpful with the process. Honest," I tell them.

We chat about a few things back home and how the weather is in New England. Life may not be terribly exciting in New Hampshire, but it's still nice to hear the local gossip.

"Well, I'm doing fine with all my classes," I interject. "I'm not really keen on astronomy but the rest of the classes are fine. I'm through with the outline of my first film and have started writing the script. I like my concept. I'm going to be really busy because I've gotta deliver a script and storyboard in the next three weeks."

"You want to share with us?" my dad asks looking eager for information.

"Actually, I'd rather wait a bit. I'm a little anxious about it and want to be sure where I am before I share anything with anyone. Sorry about that, but I know you understand," I reply.

It's true. I really don't want to tell anyone the plot until I have it all figured out. This is a big deal for me and if the story works, I hope it will be in contention for the film festival on campus.

It seems we've sort of exhausted the conversation for now and I can see they are ready to sign off. Before we hang up though, I tell them they can tell everyone in the extended family that I've come out. There's no reason to keep it a secret anymore and that way I don't have to be the one to explain it to each of them. They seem fine with it and promise to let me know when they tell people so I won't be taken off guard.

"As we said before, Brad, we're extremely proud of you, and always have been. More importantly we know you'll continue to make us proud. Being gay can be a wonderful thing for you. You can still have whatever you want. Just be the best man, best student, and best son you can be. Dad and I love you very much, Brad, and always will," she says.

There's a knock on the door and Chris walks in just as we're ready to end the session. My mom asks to chat with him for a second and I walk out into the hallway. My parents have a few moments with Chris where I can't hear what they're saying, but I'm fine with that. I'm sure they have all these protective things they need to say to him as well as to thank him for all he's done. He calls me in and steps aside so I can say goodbye.

"I'll make you proud, guys. I promise," I say as I look at both of them.

"We know you will," my dad says as they sign off.

Chris puts his arm around my shoulder as we sit on my bed together.

"They're really proud of you, man," Chris says. "You're really lucky to have such understanding and loving parents."

"I know," I say. "I'm kinda proud of me to," I tell him laughing.

I turn on the T.V. and flip the station to *Modern Family*. I feel my shoulders starting to relax. I think each day will get better. George was right. I'm starting to see the sun breaking through the clouds. Another Shakespeare quote fills my head: "A light heart lives long". The bard is with me today and I'm ready to live a long, happy life.

15

"There's special providence in the fall of a sparrow."

Last night when I was organizing things in my new room, I came across my grandfather's rosary beads. He'd given them to me a while back and I've always been so proud that he gave them to me. Looking at them reminds me of the "dream" I had about him while I was in the hospital.

I've never been all that religious. My parents raised me Catholic, but I haven't felt the need to go to church all that often since I arrived at college. I've always felt my relationship with God doesn't have to be dependent upon going to a specific place. As long as I'm a good person and try to do the right thing as often as I can, than that's what really matters. It seems though that ever since I had my moment with God, I've had a pull to come back to religion.

After taking some quiet time to reflect on what I wanted to do, I began my search. It was actually pretty easy to locate the best place to make inquiries. I did a quick internet search and found that the Episcopal Church in America seems to be one of the more accepting religions towards gays and their liturgy seems closer to what I grew up with.

There are in fact many churches in the L.A. area that specifically cater to the LGBT community, but I think that I want one that's at least a little close to the Catholic church. I'm not sure whether I'll be out with the church community, but if I'm going to spend time there, I want to be invested with a group of people I know will be understanding. Interestingly enough, the pastor at the Episcopal Church close to campus is a lesbian.

After I finish my classes, I take a short walk off campus and find the church which is literally just two blocks away. It's a rather small church community that, based on my research, has been here for many years. Reverend Katie Randall is the pastor and from what I've read is well respected. Since its mid-afternoon, I'm a little unsure of who I'll find when I ring the bell of the small rectory next to the church. I have no idea what pastors do outside of celebrating Mass so who knows if Reverend Randall will even be around.

Suddenly getting cold feet, I decide to walk into the church first hoping the building will calm me down a little. Pushing open the dark wooden doors of the small stucco church, the first thing I notice is that the inside is not all that different from the Catholic churches I know from growing up in New Hampshire. The big difference is there's no statue of Jesus on the cross, but the altar and the candles surrounding it all seem pretty much the same. I look around for a few minutes and find it seems to be deserted. Not yet ready to check out the rectory, I slide into one of the nicely padded pews and begin to pray. I start by thanking God for all the good things that have happened to me. Despite all the horrible things of the past few weeks, they have been balanced by some really good moments and I've vowed to concentrate on them. I whisper a prayer of thanks for my friends, family and actually for my former roommate, Jonathan, hoping he'll become more tolerant. It seems when I've come to God in the past, I've always asked for something. Right now I would rather thank Him.

As I finish and start pushing myself up from the crimson colored kneeler, I hear some footsteps from high heeled shoes. I turn to see who I must assume is Reverend Randall. She looks to be in her mid-forties with a kind face and short partially graying straight hair. She must work out to keep in such good shape because she is quite thin but muscular and I must say a little attractive. I know, kinda weird.

"Um, excuse me," I ask her as she crosses the front of the church.

"Yes, young man. What I can I do for you?" she asks kindly.

"Well, I was hoping I might be able to speak with you for a few minutes. I have some questions about your church. I think I might be interested in joining," I say nervously.

She gives a pleasant smile and points her arm towards her office which is a small sparsely decorated room behind the sanctuary.

"I like to keep my office door open whenever I can. Okay?" she asks.

"No, no, not at all, Reverend," I answer understanding that she may be uncomfortable locked up with a complete stranger.

"My name is Katie Randall. You can call me Reverend Katie. What's your name, young man," she says.

"It's very nice to meet you, Reverend Katie. My name's Brad Archer," I say with a little less nervousness in my voice.

"Go ahead and have a seat. So you're interested in joining our community?" she asks with her enthusiasm seeming genuine. "That's great. May I ask what has brought you to Saint Paul's?"

"Well, I'm not sure where to begin," I say trying to sound more confident than I feel at the moment. "I've spent so much of my life in hiding and not being true to myself so I'm just going to tell it outright. It's just too tiring to keep beating around the bush," I add with a huge sigh of relief. "I recently came out of the closet and it's a long story that I don't want to go into right now. I ended up in the hospital and while I was there I had a dream where God spoke to me. I'm not sure what to make of the dream, but all of this has led me here. I'm trying hard to find my way in life right now, discovering who I really am. I want my relationship with God to be a part of that and I'm hoping this church can help." There I've finally said it I think to myself as I look across the desk at her.

"Well, that's one of the most direct explanations I've heard someone tell me since I started here and it's truly refreshing," she answers with a smile. "First though you need to know that this church is fully inclusive and no one is turned away based on sexuality or gender identity. I'd like to think I'm the best example of that. It's my belief that God loves all of us, and our sexuality is gift from Him. You need not ever feel ashamed here," she goes on, leaning back comfortably in her chair and pushing back a stray strand of hair from her face.

"Why is it that your church feels this way and other denominations truly seem to hate us? I mean I've read of people preaching about the evils of gay people. One church even has a website with a streaming banner reading 'God Hates Fags'. Others would like to put us behind an electric fence rather than let us live our lives. There just seems to be so much hate and intolerance."

I can see the concern on her face and it reminds me of George when I first met him.

"Here's the deal, Brad. There are a lot of conflicting views on sexuality in the Bible and there's no question that the Bible does talk about "homosexuality" in a negative light. I'm sure you're familiar with the Old Testament phrase "thou shalt not lie with mankind, as with womankind: it is abomination?" "she asks.

I nod in agreement. I had actually heard this one long before I even started coming out. With all the discussions and confrontations about marriage equality, many people throw out that phrase over and over in their defense of traditional marriage.

"So many people have discussed what that really means but in the end, it doesn't really matter. Religion, like anything else, needs to evolve with time, but it's going to take some groups much longer than others." She stops for a moment and leans forward in her chair. "That's just something you're going to have to accept, Brad, or you have the option to bring about change. An interesting thing to remember is that the Bible says a lot of things are abominations. Homosexuality is just one of them. Eating shell fish or planting two different seeds next to each other are common examples. The Bible even promotes slavery, but we don't do that anymore, do we? It's all about evolving and I'd like to think that religion and the world are better when that happens."

Reverend Katie pushes her chair back and she stands behind the desk as she gathers some papers, "I have to get to the hospital to visit some patients from the parish. "Here," she says. "Why don't you take this pamphlet about Saint Paul's and maybe come to services this Sunday. I'll be the celebrant at all the Masses. Sometimes Reverend John from across town helps out, but not this weekend," she says pointing to a poster behind her with the Mass schedule.

"Thank you, Reverend Katie; I really appreciate you taking the time to meet with me. I'll do my best to make it on Sunday. You know, I really hope this community will help me get closer to God. I've felt sort of removed from Him in the last year or so."

She extends her hand and shakes mine warmly. "I hope so too, Brad. Good luck, and thanks for coming by."

As she turns to close the office door behind us, I stop her. "Um, Reverend Katie. I heard you say you were going to the hospital. I was wondering if maybe after a few weeks of coming to the church here, I might be able to come with you to the hospital. I have some volunteering hours I sort of need to do and I think I might like to commit to some time at the hospital."

Reverend Katie turns and smiles at me. "Well, I can't promise anything right now, but maybe in a few weeks we can work something out. It was a pleasure to meet you, Brad. Oh, and by the way, we also have a number of groups for young LGBT people here and I think you'd probably fit in nicely. Take care, Brad."

"Thanks, Reverend Katie," I say.

I follow her out of the office as she locks the door behind us.

I look at the church one last time before I leave. I feel good about what just happened. I'm glad to have God in my life again. I've let a lot of people into my life lately and now it's time for me to get reacquainted with J.C. More and more I feel that I can be gay and be happy. Like the Flintstones, I'm ready to have a gay old time I think to myself, smiling as I imagine Fred and Barney cruising around Bedrock.

16

"To be or not to be"

After all the anxiety coming out, it was finally time for me to enjoy myself. I think I deserve it. And what better way to do that than just hanging out with friends, especially Laura and Chris. For the past few days we've been inseparable. Going to the movies, mini golf; shopping. Tonight we decide to splurge and head down to Korea town and sing some karaoke.

Riding over with Laura and Chris, I can see they're smiling at me more than usual.

"What's up with the two of you?" I ask suspiciously.

"We're just happy that's all. It seems like you've finally truly accepted yourself," Laura says enthusiastically.

"We have the real Brad back and I for one am thrilled. The last Brad was quite the tight ass. Hey, on second thought, maybe that's a good thing," Chris says laughing out loud.

"Ha...ha...ha you two. Laugh now, but you won't be all smiles when my amazing singing skills outdo the both of you," I reply with confidence. I actually have pretty decent vocals.

After circling the block twice, Laura finds parking on the street pretty close to the bar and checks out the signs to make sure we're legally parked. You never know in L.A. What can look like a free spot is often in a zone with an obscured parking ban sign.

Karaoke in Korea town is a little different than other kinds of karaoke. The bars are very chic and highly stylized. Everyone who works there is friendly and the atmosphere has a definite Asian feel. All the songs are listed in English and Korean.

We had decided earlier to chip in and get a room for ourselves. The problem is we got here a little early and the room is still occupied, but there's a bar out in the main room and a stage for anyone to sing on. I watch Chris as he walks over and writes something down. He comes back and whispers something into Laura's ear and she smiles.

Getting up from the bar, she walks over to me. "Sweetie, you, me and Chris are going to sing a song together. Okay?" she says with a wicked twinkle in her eye.

A little nervous, I say, "I thought we were just gonna to wait for the room. What song have you two roped me into?

"Now, Brad, that would ruin the surprise if I told you. Get ready though because we should be on stage in a few minutes."

"If you say so, Laura. Just do me a favor though, you two, don't make an ass out of me," I plead.

"I promise nothing," Chris shouts running over to me and tousling up my hair. "I know what song we're singing, dude, and I know you're gonna love it. Promise."

I know I shouldn't be drinking, but I walk over to the bar and order a Kamikaze shot which the cute bartender offers to do with me. A tad confused, I stare back at him. I'm not sure why he offers to do a shot with me. Is he hitting on me or is he just looking for a good tip? My gaydar isn't too honed yet so I'll just assume he's straight and wants the tip. We do the shot and simultaneously slam the glasses down on the bar. It's pretty smooth and I don't choke it back. I don't have much time to think about it, or the bartender, when suddenly I hear the announcement over the speakers.

"Okay, everybody, it's time for the Archer trio. Chris, Laura and Brad, you're up," the announcer says with all the excitement associated with his profession.

Suddenly out of nowhere, Laura runs up to the bar and grabs my hand.

"It's time," she screams dragging me from the bar.

"Wait, wait; I haven't paid my bill yet," I protest suddenly really unsure of what lies ahead.

Laura quickly drops a ten on the bar and drags me to the stage. She then proceeds to take one of those 10 gallon cowboy hats and drops it on my head. A 1920's top hat is handed to Chris and she grabs a wig that would make Cher proud. Just as I think it can't get any more embarrassing, Chris grabs one of the three mics.

"Before we get started, we would like to dedicate this song to one of our co-singers. Brad, with everything you've gone through in the last few weeks, just remember you'll always be our Rose. She's the dumb one right," he says turning to me, flashing that million dollar smile.

The screen comes up and I see the name Andrew Gold as the singer and writer and that really means absolutely nothing to me. Very quickly my palms start sweating and my shoulders tense up all over again until I see the song title, *Thank You For Being a Friend*, and there's no way I can hide the smile that's now planted across my face. I'm not sure I know the whole song, but when it starts I realize I know it.

When I was a little kid, I used to watch reruns of the *The Golden Girls* all the time. Like most 80's sitcoms, I'm sure at the time I didn't get all the jokes, but enough of them made me laugh to keep watching. Now the show is on multiple networks and I watch it all the time. As I sing the song, I'm reminded of what the show was all about. It dealt with all kinds of issues, but in the end, it was always back to those four women in that house supporting one another in any circumstance. I know why Laura and Chris chose this song. It's to remind me never to forget they're there for me. I suppose to some degree your friends become your family when you leave home and go away to college.

Once the song is finished, Chris turns to me and puts his hand on my shoulder.

"We're proud of you, man," he says and I know he means it. Before leaving the stage, we do a group hug just like the Golden Girls.

Over the next few hours we sing to our hearts' content. About 10 friends join us in the private room and we sing everything. Everyone's egging me to sing "It's Raining Men", but I decline and sing Donna Summer's "Hot Stuff". With my inhibitions lowered now after having sung on a stage in front of complete strangers, "Hot Stuff" is easy. I even thrust my hips forward for emphasis. I'm living life now. All the bullshit from the past few weeks is melting away.

The ride back to campus is pretty uneventful. Remembering to take it easy with the whole drinking thing, I had decided my first shot was going to be my only drink so I was the designated driver for the trip back. After dropping Chris and Laura off at their dorms, I head back to mine. Walking into the room it finally feels like my own. Getting undressed and into my sleep pants and a tee shirt, I turn on my laptop and decide I can spend a few minutes to working on finishing up my script for my film. This film is really important to me. It's the film that'll help me focus on what I really want to be as a filmmaker. I have to write, direct and edit this project myself, but it's not a solo project by any means. When I made the decision to tell this story, I knew I would need to speak to some people at the LGBT Center on campus.

Once I had the outline for the film, I spoke with George to see whether he thought the concept was a good one.

"You do understand, Brad, that this may out you to a whole heck of a lot of people on campus," he said.

"Yeah, I know but this is the story I want to tell. I spoke with my professor just to make sure I wouldn't be rattling any cages by telling this story. She explained there were virtually no restrictions on making films as long as there was no nudity and nobody was physically hurt or slandered in the process. I'm pretty sure I can comply with that."

"Brad, I've been here a long time and have attended every one of the film festivals and it seem so many of the stories are about depression and suicide. From your outline though it seems you're taking a totally different approach. Make your film unique and more important, Brad, by doing so I think you'll impress a lot of people around here." George then paused for a few moments before looking me squarely in the eyes. "I know a few acting students here that might be interest in helping you out. If you want, I'll set you up with them."

"I'd love that, George. I would obviously prefer to have actors that have gone through something like what I'm telling but in the end, I'm just looking for good actors."

"Obviously you'll want to find the best actors you can, but I certainly have a few kids you may want to talk to. You do this right and who knows where this thing could go."

I suppose I should explain the story I've come up with. Ever since I started the process of coming out, I've actually thought about how others have dealt with it and what it all means to the young and gay in our country. There's no question that I've been bullied by my roommate and I know I'm not alone. I wondered how others have dealt with the constant bombardment of being hassled by people around them. I know there have been a lot of personal stories with the *It Gets Better* campaign and I think that's great, but my film is meant to be a little different.

My plan is to have the film take place in "everywhere'sville" so the audience has no stereotypical concepts about the environment the young man is in. Location can be extremely important when it comes to how the audience reacts. Different areas of the country have very different feelings towards gay people. If I can have the location be non-descript, then the audience won't have any preconceived notion of how to feel either for my protagonist or anyone else for that matter.

The story will revolve around four different young adults and their coming out experiences. One girl is afraid to tell her parents because she fears getting kicked out of the house. The second is worried to tell his best friend for fear that he may lose her as a good friend. The third is afraid of how God will judge him when it comes to his sexuality and the final young man knows he needs to tell his longtime doctor, but is afraid of all the things the doctor might tell him about being gay as well as if he may judge him for his lifestyle. Each of these stories will be connected by the use of a chat room where the characters meet every night. Without physically meeting, they will become a support network for each other. The film will view specific circumstances in their lives that the audience will view in real time and then they will come back to the chat room and discuss what happened with the group. I'm hoping the outcomes will differ greatly enough so the audience will never be sure what's going to happen to the characters. It's important to me to create a bond among these people while telling a moving story that may change the way some people view gays.

With the outline finally finished, I have to create a script, which I already have mapped out in my head, and then present it to my professor for approval. My next step is to assemble a crew. This shouldn't be too much of a problem with all the kids I've worked with in the film program. My friend

John does great camera work, and Stacey's pretty amazing with lighting. With some prodding I should be able to get Robert to do sound. Once the crew is assembled and I'll find the right actors, we'll start shooting over a few days and then get to post production. Because the story came to me a little late in the semester, I'm having to play catch-up, but if I can hash out the script pretty quickly, then I'll be back on track.

For a few hours I work on the script and get a pretty polished draft done. Having met my goal for the evening, I set the lap top on my desk, rub my eyes, and lie on my bed for a few moments, just relaxing and thinking about nothing. I'm suddenly jolted back to reality, when my pants start to vibrate and I grab my phone from my pocket. Looking at it, I notice it's a text. A text from Dylan, the nurse from the hospital.

A few days after I got out of the hospital, I didn't want to lose a chance of at least becoming friends with Dylan so I texted him my number. He responded right away asking how I was doing and if I was still getting the headaches. I told him I was doing much better. Over the next few days we continued to chat via text and online. It was all very sweet and innocent. Having only known him during my brief time at the hospital and through texting, I wasn't quite sure where this friendship was headed 'til I saw the most recent text from him.

> *Have night off tomorrow…Don't want to be too bold*
> *but would u like to go to dinner?*

God, I wasn't expecting that and I find my palms starting to sweat. Despite everything I've done since I came out, this would really be the first date I've had with a guy. I don't

153

count Kevin because that ended up not really being a date like I'd hoped. Even my dates with girls have been nothing spectacular so at least the bar's not set too high.

I've been working my ass off with this film and the rest of my classes for the last week and I'm actually finally caught up so why not go out.

Sure. Sounds great. What time?

How about 6:30? Let's meet at Rusty's ok?

Rusty's is a pub on campus. It's not the best place for me to meet since I'm not fully out of the closet, but what hell, I don't want to let this chance go by.

Rusty's it is. See you tomorrow.

I grab the charger next to my bed, plug in my phone and close my eyes hoping to dream of what tomorrow will bring.

The next day is pretty uneventful except for wondering about how the date with Dylan will go. After classes I return to my room to get ready. At about 5:30 I take a quick shower. I like the privacy of my own room and now I have more space to hang my shirts which I've actually ironed so I don't even have to scramble to get a decent one. I try to pick a shirt that makes me look good without giving much of a vibe. I pull a long sleeve blue button down out of the closet and decide to leave the two top buttons unbuttoned and splash on a little Calvin Klein cologne. Here we go, Brad Archer.

Before I leave the room, I notice a package laying by the door that I got yesterday and forgot to open. With a little time to spare, I get out the utility knife my dad gave me as he was leaving the dorm when I first came here – it's one of the best gifts I've ever gotten I might add – and slice open the tape. Opening the box, there's something wrapped in tissue paper with a card on top. I open the card first.

> *Brad, you are truly a caring and loving young man and we are so proud of you and everything you have done so far in school and in life. We are also so proud that you came out to us in such a brave way. Everyday you continue to become a more extraordinary young man. Please remember we will always love you and there's someone here who has missed you very much. We know he'll help you remember all those good times when you were a kid.*
>
> *Love,*
> *Mom and Dad*

This is just another example of why I love them so much. They must have mailed this literally the day after I called them. I remove the wrapping paper to find one of my favorite stuffed animals I had as a little kid, a tattered yellow terry cloth teddy bear with painted eyes, nose and mouth. He was always special to me because he was one of the only things my older brother had before he died that was passed on to me.

I carefully take him out of the box and give him a warm hug. Reading the letter again and holding Mr. Bear makes me feel warm inside. I'm quickly taken out of my reverie though as I glance over to the clock on my desk. After a quick check in the mirror, I make a mad dash out of the dorm towards Rusty's and my date.

17

"The very instant that I saw you did My heart fly to your service"

I head quickly over to Rusty's. It's in the middle of campus and I should get there about ten minutes before Dylan does. It's a Sunday so there shouldn't be a lot of people in the popular pub/restaurant. Rusty's is pretty much like most pubs in the city, but one of its unique aspects is a stage where bands from the university play during the week.

Once inside I see Sandy, one of the first friends I made when I got to campus. She and I went through freshman orientation together and shared two classes last semester. We've stayed casual friends this semester as well. She pretty with blond hair and a killer smile.

"Hey, Sandy, how the heck are you? Still waitressing at Rusty's I see," I say as I walk over to her pay station where she's ringing up a customer's bill.

She runs from behind the counter and gives me a big hug while her eyes appraise me giving me the once over.

"Still here and well, well, well don't you look adorable tonight," she says with a smile. "I haven't seen you in a few months, Brad. What've you been up to?"

"Actually a lot, but I'm afraid it'll have to wait for another time, kiddo. I'm meeting someone in a few minutes," I say.

"Great. Let me just give this bill to the customer and I'll get you a seat," she says smiling.

After placing the bill on the table, she grabs two menus from the holder next to the register.

"So where'd you like to sit then?"

"I'd like a table over there. The one in the corner if that's cool?"

"That's sort of in no man's land, Brad. You sure you want to be way over there?" she says screwing up her face in a quizzical way that's always looked endearing on her.

"Yup, that's exactly where I want to be."

"No problem, hon," she says as she seats me and immediately brings over a Diet Coke. She knows me better than I thought. Sipping the soda, I start to go over in my head what the hell I'm going to talk about with Dylan. I want to keep it casual, but I really don't know anything about him either. Just don't make an ass out of yourself, Brad, I tell myself and then remember, crap he's seen my ass! Hope that's not going to be a part of the conversation.

A few minutes after 6:30, I see Dylan walk in. Wow, he's even cuter than I remembered. I pretty much remember most of what happened in the hospital, but for some reason I haven't been able to get a firm picture of him in my head.

Seeing him in the flesh, even as far away as he is, reminds me why I thought he was so attractive. He's about 5'10" and has what I believe is called a swimmer's build. He obviously goes to the gym quite a bit. He has short dark brown hair and brown eyes. He had mentioned in one of his texts that he's a few years older than me, but looking at him now he looks younger. He's wearing tight jeans and a plain red tee shirt. I like the casual look he has. In fact, I feel a little over dressed, but there's nothing I can do about that now. Okay, settle yourself down, Brad.

He walks over to Sandy and I see her pointing in my direction. Standing up, I wave and smile. I start rubbing my hands together like I always do when I'm anxious. I look down at my hands and stop immediately. Stay cool, Brad. Relax, I tell myself. You've already met him and you know he likes you. Just breathe. Damn, I wish I had Chris' confidence right now.

As Dylan walks over to the table, I stand up, as I suppose I would if I was with a girl. He comes over to my side of the table and gives me a warm hug. I hug him back even though it feels a little unexpected.

"Sorry, about that, Brad. I'm a hugger. I tend to do that with all my friends," he says noticing my reaction.

"No problem at all. I like hugs," I say trying to sound casual.

"Good. So tell me, how are you feeling? It's been a little while since I saw you in the hospital. You look pretty recovered to me. In fact you look great," he says with a bright white smile that could be in any ad for Crest white strips.

"Uh, well, uh, thanks. So do you," I stammer hoping I'm not coming across quite as bad as I feel I am.

"Sorry, Brad. I know we're pretty much meeting for the first time. I apologize if I come across as being a little forward," Dylan says as he slides into the chair across from me.

"No, not at all. I appreciate the compliment. Yeah, I'm feeling pretty good. I had headaches for a week or so and the first few days were pretty bad, but I think it was around the third day that the pain started to go away."

"Did you ever come back for a follow-up visit?" he asks.

"Yeah, I actually did at the end of the week. The forms said I should go and see Dr. Hollingsworth. I was actually hoping you'd be there, but I guess it was your day off. The doctor said I was fine," I say, finally starting to feel more comfortable.

"Whew. Glad to hear it, Brad. Hey, do you mind if I check the back of your head just to be sure there aren't any bumps," he asks matter of factly.

Just doing his job I think as I reluctantly say sure. I turn the chair around and he moves toward me so my back is facing him. Although this seems pretty inappropriate for a first date, I have to admit it feels good. I even start to get a little aroused from his hands running through my hair. After a few seconds, he stops.

"Looks like you're pretty much back to normal. Not that I'm a doctor...yet. But I think you're going to be just fine," he says.

"Well that's good to hear," I say faking a deep sigh of relief. "You want to take a second and look at the menu so we can order?" I ask not knowing what else to say.

"Sure," Dylan replies as he picks up one of the plastic encased menus Sandy left at the table.

A few moments later Sandy notices we've put our menus down and heads over to the table.

"So, fellas, what can I get you?" she says enthusiastically.

"I'll have a cheeseburger, medium, with curly fries. They're always pretty good here," I say.

"Sounds good to me," Dylan chimes in. "I'll have the same and a Diet Coke as well.

"Sure thing, hun; you guys are pretty easy customers," Sandy says as she grabs the menus from Dylan.

Walking away, she turns and winks at me and I'm guessing that means I don't really need to come out to her. Maybe this'll be the way I can tell a lot of people. They'll just find out. I wonder if that's okay though? God, I wish there was a *Coming Out for Dummies* guidebook. It'd make this whole thing so much easier.

"So, Brad, I don't really know all that much about you besides your medical history and that backside exposure. Don't be embarrassed. Just trying to break the ice a little, man," he says with a smile.

I breathe in and let out a deep breath. "Well, I suppose that eases the tension a little. You actually know a lot more about me than I do about you, but I suppose it's fine that I go first. What do ya wanna know?"

"Well, for starters what's your major and why'd you choose it?"

"Film – I'm a film major. I've loved movies as far back as I can remember. Every time I go to the theater I have this feeling that I'm going to be moved in some way or another," I tell him. "And I usually am."

"Give me an example," he says.

"I'll give you two," I say with a smile. "When I watch *Raiders of the Lost Ark*, it gets my blood pumping and I get energized. It moves at such a fast pace that all the audience can do is jump in for the ride and that's what makes it a perfect film to me," I continue, hoping he understands.

Smiling he says, "Okay and the other one."

"Well this one is coming from a completely different direction – *Singin' in the Rain*. Yes, I like musicals. I like all kinds of movies and *Singin' in the Rain* has some of the greatest dance numbers I've ever seen. By the way did you know that Debbie Reynolds had never danced professionally before that movie?" I say with excitement in my voice.

Laughing he says, "I have to say I didn't know that."

"But the most important thing I think is that it has what I believe to be the best depiction of love ever on screen."

"Really? I know the movie and I think I know what you're talking about, but I want to hear it from you," he says.

"It's pretty simple really. When Gene Kelly's character, Don Lockwood, says goodnight to Kathy, Debbie Reynolds, it's pouring outside. She says something like he needs to get inside to protect his voice because they'll be filming soon, but he tells her that to him it feels as if the sun is shining down. They kiss and it's simple; beautiful. It's perfect. The second he walks out into the rain and closes the umbrella, you know he's in love. No man would dance that long in the rain unless he's in love," I say with a small sigh. "To me a scene like that represents the joy of being in love. Good movies show us those things. They make us laugh, cry, scream or just escape. Sorry, that was a long answer to your question," I say semi-apologetically.

"No, no, that's the kind of thing you want to hear when you ask someone what their major is. It's nice to hear how passionate you are about what you're studying. I feel the same way. Mine's just a little more simple and corny," he says leaning back comfortably in his chair. "I really just like helping people. I always have. If I can help someone feel better after they've seen me, then I've done my job. That's why I'm finishing up my nursing degree and going to med school in the fall. I realized when I was studying nursing that what I really wanted to be was a doctor. Not much more to it than that."

Right after he finishes the sentence, Sandy brings over the food and gives me a little punch on the shoulder. We take our time eating so we can enjoy each other's company. For the next hour or so we just get to know one another. He asks a little about my diabetes and I share a few of my stories. For about twenty-five minutes, we talk about general things in our lives, but we finally get to the more personal stuff. I share with him most of the experiences I've had over the last month including my rather terrible first sexual experience with a guy and even tell him about the episode with Harvey Bobson. In trying to relieve the tension, I do mention how great my friends and family have been throughout and soon I'll learn that Dylan was not one of the lucky ones who had a good coming out experience with his family. Although his friends have been extremely supportive, his parents have not.

"When I was around sixteen, I had a secret boyfriend in high school. You see, I grew up in a small town in Kansas and we really had to keep everything very secret. One day when we were studying in my room, we were just doing what normal hormonal teenagers do. I closed the door, but there were no locks on the bedroom doors because my father believed that anything anyone of us did could and should be done with a door open. We had just started to kiss when my dad walked into the room. He literally kicked Tommy out and hit me pretty hard in the face knocking me to the ground. I was told never to see Tommy again and while I was under their roof never to do something as blasphemous as he had just witnessed."

"Knowing how Dad reacted, Tommy and I started meeting in secret. It was the only way. It was hard on both of us and after a little while we just couldn't do it anymore. I never forgave my father for that, but he has also never seen me with anyone since. Once I graduate from college, I'm home free and don't have to give a shit what he thinks, but right now my scholarship only covers part of my tuition and I need to make sure he keeps paying for school," he says with a deep sense of sadness in his voice.

"I'm so sorry, Dylan. I can't even imagine how awful it must have been for you."

"You know what? You deal with it," he answers with resignation. "It's another reason why I want to be a doctor. I might not be able to heal people's emotions, but I can make a difference in their lives and heal some of their sickness. It'll be another example of how I'm not my dad," he says with confidence.

"What about your mom? And do you have brothers and sisters?" I ask, hoping this chapter in his story shows more understanding.

"You know that's the funny part of it all. I know my mom's pretty okay with it. She even wrote me a letter telling me so, but the hold my dad has over her doesn't allow her to contradict him. She thinks he may come around some day. I hope he does, but I'm not holding my breath. I did tell both my brother and sister. It took awhile for them to be cool with it, but they're pretty supportive now. Just my dipshit dad that's the problem," he continues running his fingers through his hair and obviously still upset. "Boy, I'm carrying on. Sorry about that. My life sounds like it's awful, but truth be told, I have a lot of friends here and I'm studying what I love. Can't do much better than that."

I look straight into his eyes and say, "It mustn't have been easy sharing this story, Dylan. It means a lot to me that you did."

"It's all part of the tapestry that's my life. There's good and there's bad. You just have to make sure the good's always outweighing the bad," he says.

As I look up, Sandy's heading over to the table to settle the bill. "All right, you two, my shift's about to end. If you don't mind settling, that'd be nice," she says laughing a little.

Dylan quickly grabs the bill before I can get to it.

"I don't have much now, but someday I'm going to be a rich doctor, and I think I can afford this one. It's on me," he says with a smile.

"Well if you insist," I reply. "Hey, would you like to go for a walk," I ask hoping to prolong the date as long as possible.

"Burning off a few of those calories wouldn't be such a bad thing," he says as we walk out of Rusty's together.

Starting to walk through the campus I realize that my shoulders are relaxed and I'm pretty calm.

As we walk away from the pub Dylan says, "I have a place we can go to. Do you mind a little adventure?"

"You know, Dylan, I watch a lot of *Dexter* so as long as you promise not to cut me into little pieces and dump me in the ocean I'm good," I tell him with a laugh.

We walk across campus and finally end up at the same oak tree I was sitting under just a short time ago.

"You know this is one of my favorite places too," I say.

We sit down under the large tree resting our backs against it as a warm breeze moves past us.

"Do you mind if I hold your hand," he asks in such a polite manner that I find myself smiling.

"Um...yeah that's cool."

"I know you're still coming out and I don't want to push anything. If it's okay with you, let's just take it slow and see where it goes," he says warmly.

Our fingers interlock, my hormones start to energize and I feel the sexual energy running through me. Fighting the feeling, I say, "Taking all of this slow is the best thing I could have heard tonight. For awhile now my life has been all about rushing into things. I really like the idea of us taking our time. Sort of like the old-fashioned courting," I answer hoping he doesn't think I'm too corny.

He takes his hand from mine and puts his arm on my shoulder as we look at the skyline of L.A.

"I hope this isn't too forward for your 'old-fashioned courting style'," he whispers into my ear. He gently moves my head towards his and brings his lips to mine. Slowly our lips meet. I feel a strong energy between us. Part of me wants to rush into this but being the inexperienced one, I let him take the lead. He opens his mouth and so do I. Our tongues touch and my arms are now wrapped around his. A few more minutes of this and then he gradually pulls away.

"Wow, you're a great kisser, Brad. Are you sure you're really new to all of this?" he asks with a quiet laugh and smirk.

"Scout's honor," I reply.

"Well then I can't wait 'til the next date. Why don't I walk you back to the dorm? That sounds like the old-fashioned thing to do," he says with a laugh.

Getting up, he takes my hand. As we walk through campus, I suddenly get nervous thinking people will see me holding his hand. Shaking off the fears, I hold his hand even tighter as we walk to the front of my dorm.

"Um, would you like to come up for a few minutes?" I ask.

"I'd love to, but I think I should be heading home. If I come in, we'll probably end up right where we shouldn't be. You're a really great guy, Brad, and I really want to go out again," he says.

"Yeah, I guess you're right, Dylan. Hey, are you free in the next few days," I ask hoping my voice doesn't sound as desperate as I think it does.

"Yup, I am. I'll give you a call, Brad."

Before he walks away, he looks around him to make sure we're alone and then leans me against the wall of the building and kisses me passionately and then moves away. As he turns to leave, he gives me a quick seductive smile and one last wave.

For the first time ever I'm happy about a date. I feel there could be something here. I want to make this work. I close my eyes and feel as happy as Don Lockwood must have felt when he kissed Kathy Seldon and then danced to his heart's content in *Singin' in the Rain.*

I'm ready for the next step. If it were raining right now I know I'd be dancing.

18

"I would not wish Any companion in the world but you"

After my date with Dylan I'm on an emotional high. It feels amazing to have had a date with someone that actually went well. Since I can remember, I haven't felt at all comfortable on a date – ever. I could just never make the right connections with girls (At least I now know why that was). But this time it really was different. The next day Dylan called and we talked for almost an hour. Just talking about random things. The conversation just flowed so easily. Finally I know what other people had been experiencing in high school and college when they said they made a connection with someone.

Today I decide to head over the Center and talk with George. Walking over, I feel something different about myself. I'm smiling and I'm completely relaxed. My shoulders are down and I'm not wringing my hands. I'm comfortable and it feels good. Sure, I know it might be just the early excitement of meeting a new guy and who knows what the future will hold, but right now I have a right to be happy and I'm going to allow myself to enjoy it.

I bound up the stairs two at a time and almost bolt into George's office only noticing right before I open my mouth that he's on a call. I slowly back out of the office bumping into a potted plant on my way and take a seat in the hallway. I feel like I'm going to burst.

A few moments later I hear him put the phone down. "Come on in, Brad, and maybe you can put my ficus plant back on its feet," he says.

I quickly put the plant upright and all but skip over to the chair across from him.

"Well, well, well, you seem to be in quite a good…"

But before he can finish the sentence, I blurt out, "I'm amazing! I went out on a date and it was perfect and so was he!"

"That's wonderful, Brad. How'd the two of you meet?"

"Well actually he's going to med school in the fall and he was assigned to the doctor who tended to me when I was in the hospital a few weeks ago. We seemed to make a connection when I was there and he gave me his number. We chatted a little after that and then finally he asked me out and you know what they say…'The rest is history!'"

I'm so excited and wrapped up in my story, I fail to notice Kevin standing in the doorway.

"So, Lothario, when's the next date going to be," Kevin asks, arms folded comfortably across his chest and smiling almost as broadly as I am. I get up out of my chair and give him a little hug. After which he heads over to the chair by the bookcase and I back into the chair in front of George's desk.

"It's great to see you, Kevin. I'm really glad you're here. Well, one of the main reasons I came here is as you are both keenly aware, I have very little experience with the gay dating scene and certainly know nothing on handling a second date. I have absolutely no idea what to do next, guys. I could really use some help. I did a little reading online, but everything I find seems to contradict the last article I read."

"Good lord, I would have hoped by now you wouldn't be so dramatic about everything," Kevin says as he pulls his chair closer to mine.

"Remember, the more you allow stress to control you, the less likely your next date will go well. Just take a deep breath and plan another dinner with him," Kevin advises.

"Brad, it really can be that simple. There's no need to make it be something big. Try and enjoy yourself," George confirms.

"So, did he make you feel comfortable during your dinner?" Kevin asks.

"Actually, yeah he did. I think he noticed that I was a little nervous, so he did his best to keep me at ease," I reply.

"Then why would the second date be any different, Brad? I mean you came in here a few minutes ago elated. Stay that way! Good lord, you met a guy. That's a wonderful thing. Enjoy the moment. I'd kill to have a date right now," laughs Kevin.

Looking back and forth between the two of them, I finally let myself relax and smile at Kevin knowing he's right.

I mean I knew it all along. I just needed someone to tell me. Looking at Kevin I hesitate and then answer.

"Hey… um, Kevin. Would you be interested in starring in a film I'm making? I'm also going to be needing a consultant to the other actors and I couldn't think of a better choice, than you. This is my way of thanking you for everything, by putting you to work of course," I say laughing.

"Moi? I would be honored to star in your film, Brad," he says taking a little pre-Oscar bow.

"Well, George has said he'd look over the script and help me with any inconsistencies, so that'll be a big help as well," I tell him as George nods in acknowledgement.

"You know I'm a theater minor so that couldn't hurt," he says in a faux French accent.

"You mean you're a gay guy that studies theater? You must be an anomaly," I say laughing. "Later this week I'll text you, Kevin, and we can meet to go over the script. Thanks for the help, guys. I know I can be a Debbie Downer sometimes and it means a lot that you've been here for me," I say getting up out of the seat. "And sorry George, I hope I didn't do any mortal harm to that plant of yours."

"It'll be fine, Brad, and thanks for sharing your good news. It sure beats some earlier conversations we've had," he says as he gets up and gives me a quick hug before I head out.

I leave the Center and head across campus to the Cary Grant Theater. It looks like a few of the major classes are getting out now and I'm hoping at least two of the people I need to see will be around.

As a large group of students leave the building, I spot James and Phillip, two of my good friends, and corner them as they exit the building together. It doesn't take too much persuading to get them to take roles in my film. James is gay, but Phillip isn't, but he's open minded enough to say yes anyway after I give them a quick plot summary.

"Any chance to have some screen time is good for me," he says smiling.

Now I just need to get Derek on board. I find him outside of one the classrooms just inside the building.

"Hey, Derek, what's up, my man?" I say enthusiastically.

"What's up, Brad? I haven't seen you in awhile. What's happening?"

"You know the usual. Anyway, I'm making a movie for my film class and wondered if you'd be interested in being in it."

"What's it about?" he asks.

I give him the basic outline of the film. I'm less confident asking Derek. I'm friends with him, but I wouldn't call us close by any means. I did, however, see him in a small part in *Hamlet* last year and thought he was quite good. I know he'll be amazing in the role I have in mind for him if only he'll take the part.

"I dunno, man. I'm a pretty open-minded guy, and I'm completely okay with gay people. I just don't know if I want to be in something where I could be labeled something I'm not," he says with obvious concern.

"Listen, it's cool. I wanted to ask you first because I thought you were great in *Hamlet* last year. I totally understand. I'll keep you in mind for my next project," I say.

I start to walk away when he taps me on the shoulder.

"You really thought I was good in *Hamlet*?" he says with a smile.

"You were killer, man," I exclaim.

"All right, I'm in. Hey, it's acting," he says with a shrug of his shoulders.

"Thanks for doing it, Derek! Let's meet on Saturday around 1:00. I reserved one of the study rooms in my dorm. I need to get this thing rolling."

Getting my cast on board is a huge relief. I had already asked my friend Cassandra the other day for one of the roles. She was frankly a piece of cake to ask. I can now breathe a lot easier now. Between meeting with George and Kevin this morning and finishing the casting, I'm in a pretty good place right now.

Once I'm back in my room for whatever reason, I pick up the phone and start dialing Dylan's number.

"Hey, Brad, how's it going?"

"I've never done this before, Dylan, but I'm having an amazing day and I suddenly just picked up my phone and started dialing your number. It was instinctive. I wanted to share how great I'm feeling with you," I say.

There's silence on the line. Damn, I've said something wrong. God, this is so typical of me. I hope I haven't screwed this up.

"Wow. I'm really glad you called, but the fact that you called me to share how good things are going really means a lot to me. So any chance you might be free tonight?" he asks.

"I've actually got a lot of prepping I need to do for my film 'cause I have a meeting with my crew on Saturday, but I'm going to need a break at some point. How does 7:30 sound?"

"Yeah, that's perfect. I finish up around 6:00. Why don't you come by my apartment? I'll text you the address. That'll give me enough time to make us some dinner."

"Sounds great. Would you like me to bring anything," I ask.

"Nope. Just your cute, little self. See you at 7:30."

"Great. See you then," I say and hang up the phone and raise my fist in the air in triumph. My excitement, however, is short lived because if I don't move quickly, I'll be late for my meeting with my film professor. Finalizing my cast was the last thing I need to do.

With my story boards, script revisions and location scouting done, today's the day to present everything to Professor Moore for his approval. Once again my anxiety kicks in, but after looking over my notes, he approves the project and gives me a release for all the equipment I'll need for the shoot. I then rush to another meeting with my shooting crew which went as well as can be expected at this early stage in production. Everyone seems to be on board. I explain again to everyone the sensitivity of the project and that it'll be examining some tough issues, but they all seem ready for the challenge. We plan to meet again on Friday.

Back in my room I go over Professor Moore's notes and make one more tweak to the storyboard. I'm aware there are some real issues with the script, but that will take more time and concentration than I have now so I put it aside. I lay out the entire storyboard on the floor in sequential order. This allows me to simulate watching the film from page to page through the drawings. After examing the boards a few times, I sit on my bed, relaxed with the thoughts that this has the possibility to be one hell of a film. I remember Steven Spielberg saying once that filmmaking is a collaborative process and he always brought in the best people in the industry to handle the tasks at hand. I really believe I have some of the best on campus. I can feel my confidence rising and it feels good. Finally coming out has helped in so many ways. I'm certainly more focused and assured.

Picking up my script and storyboards, I place them in my film binder, which I fondly call my bible. Happy that my confidence is up, I head over to the closet to find the right thing to wear tonight. I'm not really sure what the right thing is to wear on a date like this. I finally settle on a grey button down shirt and black tight fitting jeans. I jump into the shower and shave quickly, dress and take a look in the mirror. Deciding I look fine, I spritz on a little cologne and head out the door to Dylan's.

Leaving the dorm, I glance again at the address on my phone. I've checked it out and it's only about ten minutes from my place. I've decided to leave right at 7:30. I think it's better to give him some extra time. Arriving ten minutes late isn't a bad thing. It allows me to be in a time frame that's acceptable without appearing to be over eager. I've never understood that whole protocol about when you need to arrive at a social event. Most people claim there is a range of time to arrive, but you never should arrive right on time. Ten minutes should be fine.

Walking over to his apartment gives me the time to let go of my work on the film and focus on my time on Dylan. Seeing there's no one around to commit me as a loony, I shake out my arms and hands and move my head in circles to try to calm down, but if someone does walk by, they'll think I'm an Olympic swimmer ready to start the dive sans the pool. I'll be in a straight jacket before I get another 50 feet! Tonight I've got to take things a little slow. Because I moved so quickly with my coming out, I think I've convinced myself that this is my time even though Dylan and I discussed not rushing anything. I need to look at this date like the last one but just allow myself to be a little more relaxed. He obviously likes me so maybe I don't have to work so hard.

Getting closer to his apartment, I notice a Ralph's grocery store ahead. I take a detour and grab a bunch of Gerber daisies. And why not? It feels like the right thing to do.

Coming up to his apartment building, I find his name on the list next to the intercom. I pick up the receiver and type in #192 on the keypad and wait a few minutes for the buzzing sound and the click of the door lock. After going down the wrong hallway, I finally find his apartment and nervously breathe into my hand to see if my breath is okay. Quickly I grab a mint out of my pocket and toss it into my mouth and ring the doorbell. As I wait for him to come to the door, I notice something. I'm a little nervous but not enough to do my usual hand wringing. This is a good thing.

Dylan opens the door and I have to force myself not to stare. He looks incredibly sexy. He's wearing a black button down shirt with the top two buttons undone and some very cute jeans. He looks incredible.

"Come on in, Brad," he says taking me by the hand and giving me a kiss on the cheek. The touch of his hand and his lips on my cheek are electric and I feel it coursing through me.

As he closes the door, I hand him the flowers. "So I thought I could at least bring something to the dinner," I say.

"You're so sweet," he says leaning over and kissing me on the cheek again.

"Let me put them in a vase on the table," he says as he walks over the kitchen and bends down to get a vase from the lower cabinet. "Oh, I forgot to ask if you liked chicken," he says turning around with a hopeful look.

"Yeah, I love chicken," I answer as I can't help but notice the ease at which he does things.

"Do you need any help with anything?" I ask.

"If you don't mind, I already peeled the carrots but could you cut them while I find some wine for the two of us. Red or white?" he asks.

"Not really sure. I'm not much of a wine drinker. White, I guess."

"Perfect, I have a nice Sauvignon Blanc I've been waiting to open. By the way, my roommate's gone for the evening, so it'll just be the two of us."

As I'm cutting the carrots, he hands me a glass and we clink them.

"To a wonderful evening," he says.

"Hey, how about some background music? Do you like jazz?" he asks.

"Do I like jazz? I'm a huge fan. I'm not sure I ever mentioned this, but I play the alto and have loved jazz all my life. I love Dave Brubeck and think *Time Out* is one of the greatest albums of all time and Miles…"

Before I even have a chance to finish the sentence, Miles Davis' *Kind of Blue* album starts playing in the background. There's just something about this music that always puts me at ease. He joins me on the couch and we spend a few minutes talking about blues and jazz and our music tastes. He has an extremely extensive understanding of music from classical to rap to rock. This is actually great for me. My musical knowledge is rather limited, but I've always wanted to broaden it.

"How about this," he asks. "Every time we get together, we'll introduce each other to a song or piece of music we like. Even if the other one ends up hating it, it'll still give us a chance to hear new music while we get to know each other better."

Sounds good to me," I answer. "I actually have my iPhone with me and it has one song I'm sure you know that I've loved since I was a kid."

"The iPod speakers are right over there," he says pointing to a side table at the other end of the couch. As I slide the phone in the slot, I'm suddenly nervous about playing the song and think about picking something else. I decide to let myself go for it. I'm pretty sure he'll know it, I think, as I sit next to him on the couch.

The music starts and I see his face light up and he smiles. It's "Lean on Me". A song I've loved since I was a little kid. The song for some reason seems appropriate for my life right now.

As Bill Wither's continues to sing, Dylan takes my hand and pulls me up off the couch.

"Whoa, whoa…I'm a terrible dancer," I tell him feeling my face turn crimson red.

"Well, that's good then. There's another thing I can teach you," he says. He takes my hands and puts them around his waist and brings his body towards mine. As we move to the music, I rest my head on his shoulder while trying not to step on his feet. As the song ends, I hold on for a few seconds longer. Holding him feels right. Moving back to the couch, we enjoy the silence for a moment.

The moment is broken as the buzzer sounds from the kitchen. "The food should be ready. I'll go check on it. Why don't you have a look around while I get it ready," he says.

"My bedroom is the first door on the left," he yells from the kitchen.

I walk down the hall to his room. Geez, it's impeccable. A place for everything and everything seems to match perfectly. He has a small TV that faces the bed with some blu rays underneath. The movie buff in me wants to go through each of the DVDs, but I'll save that for another time.

"Hey, Brad," he yells from the kitchen. "Can you help me with something in here?"

"Sure, no problem," I call as I walk back to the kitchen smelling some terrific food. He asks me to drain the vegetables and put them in a bowl as he gets the chicken out of the oven.

"So what kind of chicken did you make? It smells terrific."

"Well it's sort of a family recipe. We call it cheesy chicken. It has parmesan cheese, bread crumbs and some different spices. It's pretty easy to make and I haven't had a complaint yet," he says.

He sets the plates with the chicken on the table along with the carrots, a salad and a loaf of warm bread.

"I'm impressed," I say as I slide into the chair he pulled out for me.

During the meal we talk about his work at the hospital, some of the patients he's seen and what courses he's taking now. I'm impressed with his obvious dedication and discipline. He seems genuinely interested as I explain my studies and how I have to take courses in all aspects of film from film history to production classes

After dessert, an apple pie which he made sugar free, we clean up everything in the kitchen and go back to the small living area.

"Want to watch some T.V.? Any suggestions?" he asks.

"Surprise me," I tell him as I settle into the couch.

"Well, the other night you mentioned a movie I hadn't seen in a long time so why don't we do that," he says as he presses play on the remote and there they are – Gene, Debbie, and Donald all singing and dancing in the rain. I lean over and give him a quick kiss on the cheek.

"This is one of the nicest evenings I've ever had," I tell him. "Just a short time ago I couldn't even imagine having a romantic dinner with another guy and here I am and it feels so right."

I remember years ago sitting around with some friends discussing the perfect date. What I said back then is basically the night I'm having right now: sitting on the couch next to someone you care about and watching a great movie.

I lean back on the couch and slide a little closer to Dylan. I put my arm around his shoulder. He moves closer and we snuggle. Our heads move next to each other and we stay that way throughout the movie. Right now, in this very moment, everything is perfect.

19

"Be true"

Two months have passed since my second date with Dylan and like the tee shirt says "Life is Good". More on Dylan in a little bit. After I finished shooting my film, I spent hours in post production with my editor, Roger. I thought he'd be good since I'd worked with him on an earlier class project, and I couldn't have gotten anyone better for this film. It's interesting that just like in the film industry, there are people on campus that are known as being extremely talented in their fields and Roger is known for his editing skills. On the first day of editing, he let me know that I needed one day of reshoots as there were a few shots that had to come from different angles. Since I still had all the equipment, I quickly reassembled the cast and took care of that. Roger literally saved the day. Actually, everyone on the shoot was extremely professional and I believe we made a pretty special movie. What's even more exciting though is that the film has been selected to be a part of the film festival on campus in a few weeks and we've been nominated for "Best Film". And just think, it was only a few months ago that I thought about swallowing pills and ending it all because my life was never going to get any better. What a change.

But the film is just one thing. I have new friends at the Center and from time to time they've helped me when I needed a little pick me up and I couldn't have asked for better gay friends than George and Kevin. They've been supportive since the start and I know they're always here for me. Someday I hope I can be like them and help others who are struggling through the process.

Even public opinion towards gays seems to be changing so quickly. There was a time when the hatred towards our community seemed like it would never change and now some might see gay issues as the in thing. There's still far too much intolerance and hatred, but things are getting better. Being gay isn't a choice. I wish I had understood that years or even months ago. This is who I am and like the dream I had in the hospital, God made me this way. Speaking of God, I've actually started attending Reverend Katie's Episcopal church near campus. I've never been all that into religion, but ever since that dream, I've felt a need to try and make a connection with Him. I don't pretend that the dream I had was anything more than that, but it did have an impact on me. Attending Mass is something that's become extremely personal to me and Reverend Katie has been a positive influence in my life. Most of my friends don't go to church and Dylan isn't all that interested either. Going every Sunday, however, allows me the time to do something alone while also being around people who accept me for who I am and appreciate my connection with God.

Sometimes I'm amazed at all that the things that have changed since I came out. Who would have thought that coming out of the closet would allow me to become closer to God? So often it has the opposite effect. My parents are happy I'm going to church because it's always been important to them and they hope I can find and become part of a supportive community. I know they're truly happy with all I've done this year.

The second thing I always try and remember is that even if it was a choice, I don't think I'd change who I am. The process of coming out has made me a stronger person. I have a better understanding of who I am now and I how I fit in this crazy world. It's also made me realize how focused I need to be on some things and not on others. I'd also like to think it has made me more compassionate toward all people.

Now on to the best of the last two months: Dylan. I've never met anyone like him. During the first few weeks of dating, we really did take it slow. We went to the movies, saw a play and even went bowling at the alley I took Mary to. Over those weeks we also became lovers. Unlike the way Bobby treated me, Dylan was and is truly warm and loving in the bedroom. He's allowed me to gradually explore my sexuality. He's been a wonderful teacher, showing me what there is to being a good sexual, loving person. This has opened a whole new world to me that I really love. He's also taught me that labels in terms of sexual acts don't work for him. When he makes love, there are no rules except to be respectful and loving. What more would anyone want.

He's also gotten to know all my friends and they love him. He's become just one of the guys and that's been important to me. I told him early on that I couldn't lose my current friends if we were going to get serious. They always have been and are just too important to me. He feels the same way about his friends, who by the way are terrific. Not all of them are studying medicine, which is good for me. I'm not sure I could handle listening to medical stories all the time.

Laura and I have also grown closer. She's allowed me to understand what it's like to be a young lesbian on campus. We share stories all the time and she and her girlfriend Rebecca go out with Dylan and me quite often. Our coming out to one another has made us closer than I would have ever expected. We share our emotions on what it means to be gay and argue passionately why certain rights are still not afforded to us. We've even started to become politically active in promoting the rights of the LGBT community.

The phrase I keep hearing from politicians is "the right side of history." Although as a community we've had many setbacks, the positives lately are become greater and more widespread. More people openly appreciate and respect us now than ever before. It seems the momentum is finally with us.

Chris and I have become closer as well. Like Laura, he has been extremely supportive and even helped out with the film when we shot on weekends. Any fears I may have had with my attraction to him have subsided. Of course, I still love him as a friend and think he's one of the most gorgeous men I have ever met – Dylan agrees with me as well – but that's changed to something different now that Dylan's in my life.

I wasn't sure I wanted to do it as I thought it might be too soon, but last week I told Dylan that I love him. He responded quickly that he also loves me. I was so worried about my timing, but the way he responded let me know it was in fact the right time. What I felt at that moment is indescribable. I was finally expressing and receiving something that I felt was impossible not so long ago.

I've tried to put into words what a crazy ride these past months have been. I mean the love and support I've gotten from everyone is beyond measure, but more than anything, I've learned to do the most important thing of all: love myself for who I am and all that I am. It took years for me to find the person I am today. It took countless experiences, some of which were extremely negative and others that were so satisfying. The coming out process can be a roller coaster. The lows, like with Harvey Bobson and my former roommate, will never go away and the climb can be excruciatingly slow, but when you get there, it really is the best. Right now, more than ever in my life, I feel like I belong, not just in the gay community, but everywhere. I feel like I fit in life.

Yesterday Dylan and I were in the car and he was playing Mandy Moore's *Wild Hope* album. The song "Extraordinary" came on. I sat back and listened. One of the lyrics in the chorus is "now I'm ready, to be…extraordinary." That's me. I'm ready. I've worked hard to get here. I've shot a film I'm proud of, made new friends and found someone who completes me right now. Where's this all going? Will Dylan and I still be together a year from now? I don't know and I don't think that matters. It's time for me to live the moment for it will never happen again; be happy now. It's time for me to be as extraordinary as I can be and to thine own self be true.

REFERENCES

Prologue: "The fault...is not is our stars, but in ourselves"
Julius Caesar Act 1, Scene 2

Chapter One: "The play (or movie's) the thing"
Hamlet Act 2, Scene 2

Chapter Two: "Friendship is constant in all other things"
Much Ado About Nothing Act 2, Scene 1

Chapter Three: "All is the fear and nothing is the love"
MacBeth Act 4, Scene 2

Chapter Four: "I stand in pause where I shall first begin, And both neglect"
Hamlet Act 3, Scene 3

Chapter Five: "O this learning, what a thing it is!"
The Taming of the Shrew Act 1, Scene 2

Chapter Six: "I do desire to learn, sir"
Measure for Measure Act 4, Scene 2

Chapter Seven: "Let me be that I am And seek not to alter me"
Much Ado About Nothing Act 1, Scene 3

Chapter Eight: "If you wrong us, shall we not revenge?"
The Merchant of Venice Act 3, Scene 1

Chapter Nine: "Oft expectation fails, and most oft there where most it promises"
All's Well that Ends Well Act 2, Scene 1

Chapter Ten: "What's done cannot be undone"
MacBeth Act 5, Scene 1

Chapter Eleven: "Boldness be my friend"
> ***Cymbeline*** Act 1, Scene 6

Chapter Twelve: "Divinely bent to meditation"
> ***Richard II*** Act 3, Scene 7

Chapter Thirteen: "Woe to the hand that shed this costly blood"
> ***Julius Caesar*** Act 3, Scene 1

Chapter Fourteen: "Thou canst not then be false to any man" (parent)
> ***Hamlet*** Act 1, Scene 3

Chapter Fifteen: "There's special providence in the fall of a sparrow."
> ***Hamlet*** Act 5, Scene 2

Chapter Sixteen: "To be or not to be"
> ***Hamlet*** Act 3, Scene 1

Chapter Seventeen: "The very instant that I saw you did My heart fly to your service"
> ***The Tempest*** Act 3, Scene 1

Chapter Eighteen: "I would not wish Any companion in the world but you"
> ***The Tempest*** Act 3, Scene 1

Chapter Nineteen: "Be True"
> ***Hamlet*** Act 1, Scene 3

The following is an excerpt from Ryan Provencher's upcoming novel:

The Obit Writer

1

Hot, Humid And Rife With Hate

It was a particularly hot and humid April evening in Oxford, Mississippi, home of the Ole Miss Rebels, as Alwin Kershaw began his nightly routine before retiring to bed. The humidity clung to the students like a disease that had no remedy. Alwin was exhausted. He felt much more than his twenty-one years. He had spent much of the day in journalism classes and then begun his beat reporting for the university newspaper, *The Mississippian*. The frustration he had felt earlier in the day was doubled as he washed his face at the sink in the communal bathroom. Once again another article of his had been turned down by the lead editor.

Acceptance of Negroes into the University must happen, Alwin thought as he brushed his teeth. Why is it that no one can see that? It's 1952 for God's sake. The Civil War ended almost a hundred years ago! Looking into the mirror, he could see the anger and frustration that had been building throughout the entire day. If he kept this up, he'd have deep furrows in his brow before he turned thirty. Splashing cold water on his face, he tried to calm his nerves. As his father always said "Tomorrow is another day," another day to fight those hypocritical bastards at the university and make them hear his voice.

This was not the first time Alwin had been shot down for his writing. His need to find justice for the downtrodden ran deep. As a young teen he began working at the soup kitchen in a town just outside of Mobile, Alabama, where he was born and raised. It was here, summer after summer, listening to the voices of the homeless and those who were less fortunate, that Alwin began his love affair with the written word. Each day, after volunteering, he would head home and write his experiences in a black leather journal he had bought with birthday money his grandmother had given him.

I must tell their story or no one will, he would say to his mother as he set the kitchen table for dinner. She was the one who had nurtured his desire to help others. Come fall he would present those journal entries to his teachers and far too often they would claim his stories were overwrought with flamboyancy and fabrications.

"Young man, I have passed by that very soup kitchen you claim to volunteer at during your summer recess and I know for a fact these stories you share are absolutely pure fiction. They have the appearance of fantasy and believe me, no one in this community would believe such outlandish tales," Ms. Elgart would chide in her scolding manner.

But Alwin knew better than to trust this woman who must have lost her soul for teaching years ago. It was, in fact, the soul that Alwin was so interested in. Where did these people come from and why were they relegated to such a debilitating existence? What was it that brought them to this place?

Being a young man with kind facial features allowed Alwin to get close to people. He presented no threat and his flair for getting what he wanted allowed him to be accepted as a volunteer at such a young age. He would take his time getting to know the people at the soup kitchen. Even if it would often be days before he would approach an individual, he wanted, no he needed, their trust. Knowing many people there would have trust issues, he would quietly draw near to those who seemed more open and perhaps willing to share their stories. Alwin never gave any indication of wanting to write anything down until he knew he had the complete confidence of the person he was speaking with. He knew he needed to earn the trust of everyone he spoke with. It was an innate sense he possessed. One that would serve him well for decades for in journalism mutual trust is the key to success. After hours of serving food to the needy, Alwin would spend time just listening: listening to the voices of those who had been silenced by a society that had forgotten them.

Alwin, however, always kept an emotional distance from the people he spoke to and frankly everyone else in his life for that matter. He shared little and when he did, it was just those things on the surface; nothing from his own soul.

And now eight years later, very little had changed for Alwin. He still spent the majority of his time listening; observing. The opportunity to put his years of writing were now finally being put to good use. Although he had been extremely unnerved the majority of the day, he knew he was starting to wear down the staff at *The Mississippian*. He had been careful though not to ruffle too many feathers. If he made enemies of everyone, then none of his articles would ever be published. The strongest weapon he had was his writing and there was no question that everyone on the paper found him to be an extremely talented journalist. He would present various articles that were of specific interest to the student population while also covering stories of national importance, careful to not to specifically cover the rights of the Negro. Recently, he had been assigned to cover the upcoming Presidential election between Stevenson and Eisenhower.

After receiving today's rejection, once again, from the lead editor, Alwin began typing what he thought was a rather brilliant article. He had interviewed fellow students who knew people or had relatives who had served in World War II. He was interested in how those veterans had adjusted to postwar life. Once that was published, he would then attempt to smuggle in an article dealing with the clearly defined racial divide at the University. Had Alwin gone to college in New York or Boston, he doubted there would be many arguments with his subject matter. Sure, there may be the stray negative response of some bigoted students, but here in the South it was different. Throughout the region, the White Citizens Councils and the Ku Klux Klan had mobilized their efforts against the Negro population. Yet even with so much anger in his heart on this issue, Alwin still loved the South and Ole Miss. People will change he thought. But why, he wondered, did he have to wait so long for others to understand they were on the wrong side of history.

Many wondered why Alwin, a talented, young, white man, seemed to be so passionate for the rights of the Negros. Although he was not able to know or spend significant time with any of them, to Alwin, none of that mattered. Like the people he had spent time with as a child, he knew the marginalized needed protection and the color of one's skin or economic status should not matter. To Alwin, in many ways it still felt like the Civil War had never really ended for so many in the South. Too many would do anything to make sure the Negro didn't receive basic human rights. But they should. Alwin also knew they could never begin to achieve the American dream if they weren't given the chance at higher education. It seemed so simple to him, but not to the vast majority of those living in Mississippi or much of the rest of the South for that matter.

Alwin did have one secret weapon at the paper; his name was Gene Harrison. Since his first semester at Ole Miss, Gene and Alwin had been the closest of friends. Gene shared Alwin's love of history, politics and movies. Gene, a year older and now studying for his Master's degree, held more weight at the paper and also had more influence with the administration. Unlike Alwin, who was fit but still on the lanky side, Gene had more masculine features with broad shoulders and a chiseled face. They had attended the school mixers every month but rarely did either of them leave with a young lady on his arm. If Alwin believed that fighting for the rights of the Negroes was going to get him in serious trouble, it was his deepest secret, however, that might in fact get him killed.

Stacking his notes into a neat pile on his night stand, Alwin slowly drifted into sleep. The fight with the editorial staff would begin again tomorrow but now was his only time to dream of holding Gene in his arms and never letting go.

ABOUT THE AUTHOR

Ryan grew up in Hudson, New Hampshire where he spent the majority of his formative years. He then went on to study film at University of Miami. Now living in Los Angeles with his husband Scott and two dogs (Bert & Ernie), Ryan works in the motion picture business. He has also spent the last eight years volunteering at the LGBT Center where he mentors people through the coming out process. *Thine Own Self* is his first novel. www.ryanprovencher.com